WOMEN
OF
VISION

WOMEN OF VISION

Edited by

Denise Du Pont

St. Martin's Press
New York

Design by Glen M. Edelstein

Library of Congress Cataloging-in-Publication Data

Women of vision / edited by Denise Du Pont.
   p. cm.
   ISBN 0-312-02321-9
   1. Science fiction, American—Women authors—History and criticism. 2. Science fiction—Authorship. 3. Women and literature—United States—History—20th century.   I. Dupont, Denise.
PS374.S35W64   1988
813'.0876'099287—dc19   88-17671
                                                                         CIP

First Edition
10 9 8 7 6 5 4 3 2 1

For Maggie and Jacques

CONTENTS

vii

◆ CONTENTS

EDITOR'S ACKNOWLEDGMENTS

Many thanks to John Sladek for his guidance and encouragement in the beginning stages of this project. I would also like to extend my appreciation to Richard Curtis and Roberta Cohen of Richard Curtis and Associates, Inc., for their patience and support of this book. I am grateful to the authors who contributed their time and effort to make *Women of Vision* a reality.

INTRODUCTION

The science-fiction and fantasy genres have been called the literature of change. Stories of alien worlds, futuristic societies, and kingdoms of magic are more than entertainment. They comment on our lives, touch our hopes and fears, and allow us to imagine alternative ways of living with one another. Women are entering this genre in increasing numbers, changing and shaping its future.

Science fiction and fantasy allow the writer to say what cannot be said in mainstream fiction—to explore unconventional philosophies freely and see them to their conclusions, to challenge gender roles and cultural norms, whether to entertain, experiment, or be visionary.

In conceiving a book of this nature I do not mean to set women apart and add to the myth that "there are writers and then there are women writers." Rather, this book is a forum that allows the woman writer of science fiction and fantasy to comment on her work. Readers can hear the range of women's voices and understand the diversity, dimension, and intensity they contain.

Women of Vision offers the reader a chance to compare, contrast, and learn about the writer and her work. After reading a novel, one often wonders what kind of person created that storyline. What motivated the writer to pursue her line of work? The essays in this anthology address these basic questions: Why do you write? What were the obstacles (or benefits) you encountered as a woman writer? Why do you write in the genre(s) that you have chosen?

I admit to another motive for putting this book together. I wanted to learn from these successful women writers how they did it. I thought of writing as something outside the self, as an institution with absolutes, a secret formula that could be obtained if one looked long and hard enough. The result was an increasing alienation and distancing between the writing process and myself. Reading the essays changed these beliefs.

There are no absolutes, and writing begins within. If it is done correctly, the author is revealed in a very intimate way. What is inside oneself will be transmuted into popular culture and challenged by fans. It is much easier to read "how to write" books than to reveal oneself this way.

The essays in *Women of Vision* also present another dimension to the writing process: the individual author's life. Understanding the author will give us insights on how to look within her work—to examine the writing process anew.

The stories of these women's lives and work are as interesting as the tales they weave. One need not be a fan of science fiction and fantasy to appreciate what these authors have to say, for they speak a language common to all artists. *Women of Vision* celebrates their achievements.

◆

THE CARRIER-BAG THEORY
OF FICTION

Ursula K. Le Guin

In the temperate and tropical regions where it appears that hominids evolved into human beings, the principal food of the species was vegetable. Sixty-five to eighty percent of what human beings ate in those regions in Paleolithic, Neolithic, and prehistoric times was gathered; only in the extreme Arctic was meat the staple food. The mammoth hunters spectacularly occupy the cave wall and the mind, but what we actually did to stay alive and fat was gather seeds, roots, sprouts, shoots, leaves, nuts, berries, fruits, and grains, adding bugs and molluscs and netting or snaring birds, fish, rats, rabbits, and other tuskless small fry to up the protein. And we didn't even work hard at it—much less hard than peasants slaving in somebody else's field after agriculture was invented, much less hard than paid workers since civilization was invented; the average prehistoric person could make a nice living in about a fifteen-hour work week.

Fifteen hours a week for subsistence leaves a lot of time for other things. So much time that maybe the restless ones who didn't have a baby around to enliven their lives, or skill in making or cooking or singing, or very interesting thoughts to think, decided to slope off and go hunt mammoths. The skillful hunters then would come staggering back with a load of meat, a lot of ivory, and a story. It wasn't the meat that made the difference. It was the story.

It is hard to tell a really gripping tale of how I wrested a wild oat seed from its husk, and then another, and then another, and then another, and then another, and then I scratched my gnat bites, and Ool said something funny, and we went to the creek and got a drink and watched newts for a while, and then I found another patch of oats. . . . No, it does not compare, it cannot compete with how I thrust my spear deep into the titanic hairy flank while Oob, impaled on one huge sweeping tusk, writhed screaming, and blood spouted everywhere in crimson torrents, and Boob was crushed to jelly when the mammoth fell on him as I shot my unerring arrow straight through eye to brain.

That story not only has Action, it has a Hero. Heroes are powerful. Before you know it, the men and women in the wild-oat patch and their kids and the skills of the makers and the thoughts of the thoughtful and the songs of the singers are all part of it, have all been pressed into service in the tale of the Hero. But it isn't their story. It's his.

2

ways. Myths of creation and transformation, trickster stories, folktales, jokes, novels . . .

The novel is a fundamentally unheroic kind of story. Of course, the Hero has frequently taken it over, that being his imperial nature and uncontrollable impulse, to take everything over and run it, while making stern decrees and laws to control his uncontrollable impluse to kill it. So the Hero has decreed through his mouth-pieces, the Lawgivers, first, that the proper shape of the narrative is that of the arrow or spear, starting *here* and going straight *there* and THOK! hitting its mark (which drops dead); second, that the central concern of narrative, including the novel, is conflict; and third, that the story isn't any good if he isn't in it.

I differ with all of this. I would go so far as to say that the natural, proper, fitting shape of the novel might be that of a sack, a bag. A book holds words. Words hold things. They bear meanings. A novel is a medicine bundle, holding things in a particular, powerful relation to one another and to us.

One relationship among elements in the novel may well be that of conflict, but the reduction of narrative to conflict (I have read a how-to-write manual that said, "A story should be seen as a battle," and went on about strategies, attacks, victory, etc.) is absurd. Conflict, competition, stress, struggle and so forth within the narrative conceived as carrier bag/belly/box/house/medicine bundle may be seen as necessary elements of a whole that cannot be characterized either as conflict or as harmony, since its purpose is neither resolution nor stasis, but continuing process.

Finally, it's clear that the Hero does not look well

in this bag. He needs a stage or a pedestal or a pinnacle. You put him in a bag and he looks like a rabbit, like a potato. That is why I like novels: instead of heroes they have people in them.

So, when I came to write science-fiction novels, I came lugging this great heavy sack of stuff, my carrier bag full of wimps and klutzes, tiny grains of things smaller than a mustard seed, intricately woven nets that, when laboriously unknotted, are seen to contain one blue pebble, an imperturbably functioning chronometer telling the time in another world, and a mouse's skull. The bag is full of beginnings without ends, of initiations, of losses, of transformations and translations, and far more tricks than conflicts, far fewer triumphs than snares and delusions; full of spaceships that get stuck, missions that fail, and people who don't understand. I said it was hard to make a gripping tale of how we wrested the wild oats from their husks; I didn't say it was impossible. Whoever thought writing a novel was easy?

If science fiction is the mythology of modern technology, then its myth is tragic. Technology, or modern science (using the words as they are usually used, in an unexamined shorthand standing for the "hard" sciences and high technology founded upon continuous economic growth) is a heroic undertaking, Herculean, Promethean, conceived as triumph, hence ultimately as tragedy. The fiction embodying this myth will be, and has been, triumphant (Man conquers earth, space, aliens, death, the future) and tragic (apocalypse, holocaust, then or now).

If, however, one avoids the linear, progressive,

time's-(killing) arrow mode of the Techno-Heroic, and redefines technology or science as primarily cultural carrier bag rather than weapon of domination, one pleasant side effect is that science fiction can be seen as a far less rigid, narrow field, not necessarily Promethean or apocalyptic at all, and in fact less a mythological genre than a realistic one.

It is a strange realism, but it is a strange reality.

Science fiction properly conceived, like all serious fiction, however funny, is a way of trying to describe what is going on, what people actually do and feel, how people relate to everything else in this vast sack, this belly of the universe, this womb of things to be and tomb of things that were, this unending story. In it, as in all fiction, there is room enough to keep even Man where he belongs, in his place in the scheme of things; there is time enough to gather plenty of wild oats and sow them, too, and sing to little Oom, and listen to Ool's joke, and watch newts, and still the story isn't over. Still there are seeds to be gathered and room in the bag of stars.

Biographical Notes

Born in California, Ursula K. Le Guin is the daughter of the writer Theodora K. Kroeber and ethnologist/cultural anthropologist Alfred L. Kroeber. Ms. Le Guin earned a B.A. from Radcliffe College and an M.A. in French and Italian Renaissance literature from Columbia University. She was awarded a Fulbright fellowship to continue her studies.

The literary honors Ms. Le Guin has been accorded are impressive. In addition to winning four Hugo and three Nebula awards, the major literature prizes in science fiction, Ms. Le Guin has been given the Rhysling and the Boston Globe/ Hornbook awards. *The Tombs of Atuan* was named a Newbery Honor book, and her novel *The Farthest Shore* was given the coveted National Book Award in 1972. One of her stories, "The Lathe of Heaven," was made into a television movie.

Ms. Le Guin currently lives in Portland, Oregon with her husband Charles Le Guin. She has three children.

Books by Ursula K. Le Guin

Wild Oates & Fireweed (Haper & Row, 1987)

Buffalo Gals & Other Animal Presences (Capra Press, 1987)

King Dog (Capra Press, 1985)

Always Coming Home (Harper & Row, 1985)

The Visionary: The Life Story of Flicker of the Serpentine (Capra Press, 1984)

Solomon Leviathon's 931st Trip around the World (Cheap Street, 1983)

In the Red Zone (Lord John Press, 1983)

The Compass Rose (Underwood-Miller, 1982)
The Adventure of Cobbler's Rune (Cheap Street, 1982)
The Eye of the Heron (Harper & Row, 1982)
Hard Woods (Harper & Row, 1981)
The Beginning Place (Harper & Row, 1980)
Edges (Pocket Books, 1980)
Torrey Pine Reserve (Lord John Press, 1980)
Gwilan's Harp (Lord John Press, 1980)
Interfaces (Ace, 1980)
Malafrena (Putnam, 1979)
Leese Webster (Atheneum, 1979)
Three Hainish Novels (Doubleday, 1978)
The Language of the Night Wood (Putnam, 1978)
The Altered I: Ursula K. Le Guin Science Fiction Writing Workshop (Ultramarine, 1978)
Nebula Award Stories XI (Harper & Row, 1977)
The Word for World Is Forest (Putnam, 1976)
The Water Is Wide (Pendragon, 1976)
Very Far Away from Anywhere Else (Atheneum, 1976)
Orsinian Tales (Harper & Row, 1976)
Dreams Must Explain Themselves (Algol Press, 1975)
The Wind's Twelve Quarters (Harper & Row, 1975)
Wild Angels (Capra Press, 1974)
The Dispossessed (Harper & Row, 1974)
From Elfland to Poughkeepsie (Pendragon, 1973)
The Farthest Shore (Atheneum, 1972)
The Lathe of Heaven (Scribner's, 1971)

◆   *Ursula K. Le Guin*

The Tombs of Atuan (Atheneum, 1970)
The Left Hand of Darkness (Ace, 1969)
The Earthsea Trilogy (Parnassus Press, 1968)
City of Illusions (Ace, 1966)
Rocannon's World (Ace, 1966)
Planet of Exile (Ace, 1966)

◆

AGENT FIRST, ANTHOLOGIST SOMETIMES, WRITER IN THE CRACKS

Virginia Kidd

I was trying to write this piece, addressing questions that seemed to have very little to do with my life, and I found myself a little bit blocked, so I put it aside and picked up a new manuscript. It was already overdue at its publisher's, so I felt justified in shifting my priorities, just for a little procrastinatory stretch.

It was pure pleasure. The manuscript was as clean as fresh laundry, requiring only two minuscule corrections in one hundred pages. The story was deeply absorbing, so that I was drawn in on page one and never once wanted to scramble free.

When I was a fair distance into the book and thinking I should put this work aside to do the essay, I suddenly realized that what I was doing is what I was born for: to be an agent and a good enough writer to search out those who can write better than I can—and to help some of them make careers, money, reputations.

Anthologies come along infrequently. The initial idea is always enormously exciting, but by the time all the endless donkey work has been accomplished—the last procrastinator chased down, the last contract signed, and the introduction and headnotes done—the excitement has been chewed up by the months of finding time to do another job while you are taking care of the full-time job that is your career. Editing is fun, but only in spurts, while reading each contribution for the first time is a sort of heaven on earth—and the joy is not (at least for me) vicarious. It is silence, on a peak in Darien; but the moments in Connecticut (ahem) are few.

No, I am not a writer manqué. I am not a disappointed person. Being an agent is my life and my joy. It is not a career I could urge on anyone else because it is very hard work. There is something that needs to be done 168 hours a week so that you always run a little bit behind and you never get quite enough sleep. But oh, is it ever fun!

In the sense in which this question in front of me is intended, I hardly write at all, although I spend almost every minute of my waking life either at the keyboard of my word processor or dictating to a typist.

I have been seized by inspiration only infrequently.

The parallel evolution of all those strains of pouched creatures (primarily in Australia) was one such moment of inspiration, resulting in "Kangaroo Court," my novella in Damon Knight's anthology, *Orbit I*. Shortly thereafter, I sold the novella to Doubleday as the partial delivery on a book that would have been called *The Flowering Season* had I ever gotten around to finishing it. After a couple of decades, I bought the contract back. The initial excitement had expended itself and in the intervening years I had decided that there was just too much product—too many books being written and published for which there was no need, either on the part of the writer or of the reading public.

Therein lay the hang-up. I could write—there was no doubt in my mind on that score—however, I had hardly anything I really wanted or needed to say. James Blish believed fervently that writing (of fiction) is done out of clinical necessity. I believed that, too. The fit came on me remarkably infrequently, but when it did happen it took me by the scruff of the neck and shook me, giving me no peace until whatever it was was written. I liked being a driven writer, but there is no way in the world that that clinical need could be faked or forced. (There is absolutely no thrill to compare with that moment when the fingers begin to type faster and faster and the conscious mind does not know what is coming next, so that the writer is just as surprised as she hopes the reader will be by the very end of the story—in my most recent case, a short piece called "The Marathon," which you may encounter some day.)

My experience as a writer, then, is limited but real. I can respond out of my own knowledge to the specific questions one gets asked. The ideal audience: myself. I write to please me. No, I do not regard propaganda as art. Though I am a woman (and pleased to be one), feminism has played no part known to me in my writing. Feminism was still being rediscovered when I wrote my considerable body of poetry, my mainstream stories, and my small stack of science fiction and fantasy.

I know well (from first discovering it, at nine) that speculative fiction has been around for a whole lot of years, and I do believe it will be with us as long as we last. I've given it more than half a century myself. I believe that the difference between speculative and mainstream fiction is that the latter is based on the readers' givens and shores up their preconceptions, while the former is for readers who like to doubt and ask questions, to tear down assumptions—to boldly go, grammatically or not, where no one has gone before. (When I was little, I told my mother I would like to be the first person to walk on the surface of the moon. She was dumbstruck. All she could think of to say was "Why?")

How can one believe there is a female or a male writing style? As an elitist, I hold that with regard to writing that is worth reading and having written, there is style and style only. I'm talking about literature. There is also a kind of prefab or ersatz writing that has no style at all, is not memorable, and is bought by the nonthinking to assist them in passing their thoughtless time. Such writing can be distinguished by what sex it is *aimed* at—that for women gushes, that for men is too hearty—but it cannot be distinguished by the gender of the writer. It may be the stuff of best-sellers, but it is not art.

I emphatically do not regard female characters as "the other" or "alien," nor as a class. A male or a female can be portrayed as inhuman, an "other," or alien, depending on the author's intention. I model a character on what I know or believe I intuit accurately of people I know, but this may be the result of a lack of imagination on my part. I have always felt that my writing partakes of reportage; my strength is that I am neither an experimenter nor an entertainer, but a stylist. (The short story "OK, O Che," which hardly anyone has ever seen and certainly no one has ever bought, does not negate the foregoing statement. It was written in the manner of Joyce, because I can. It was Joyce who did the experimenting, though, not I.)

The true answer to "Why do you write?" is "Well, mostly, I don't—not for publication. Not often." I write science fiction (when I do) because science fiction is what most pleases me. I never encountered any obstacle *or* benefit in any part of my career as a direct result of being a woman. But my career was not to be that of a writer.

When I was a girl, in Latin class, I was deeply impressed by the fact that *ago, agere* meant *do, drive, make,* and about forty-five other possible actions. It may be (although truthfully I doubt it) for that reason that I wound up being an *agent.* Certainly, it is and has been the career for me.

It has meant everything that I am, while it does not

signify that I am a woman. Both men and women act as agents, and their styles differ, but gender neither gives one an advantage nor places any obstacle in the way. Up the individual, up with literature, down with causes.

One last word, from a Latin lover; a summing-up:

FOUND POEM

This package is sold by weight, not by volume.
Packed as full as practicable by modern
automatic equipment, it contains full net
weight indicated. If it does not appear
full when opened, it is because
contents have settled during shipping
and handling.

Biographical Notes

Virginia Kidd was born in Philadelphia and was the daughter of a printer. She attended the Berlitz School of Languages and is fluent in French, German, Italian, and Spanish.

Ms. Kidd successfully worked as a free-lance writer, ghost writer, and proofreader before establishing the Virginia Kidd Literary Agency, which is located near the banks of the Delaware River, in Milford, Pennsylvania. She was one of the founding members of the former Vanguard Amateur Press Association and is a member of the Science Fiction Writers of America, the Authors Guild, the Science Fiction Research Association, and the Academy of American Poets.

Books edited by Virginia Kidd

Edges, with Ursula K. Le Guin (Pocket Books, 1980)

Interfaces, with Ursula K. Le Guin (Ace, 1980)

Millennial Women (Delacorte/Dell/Laurel Leaf, 1978)

The Best of Judith Merril (Warner, 1976)

Saving Worlds, with Roger Elwood (Doubleday, 1973)

RETROSPECTION

Anne McCaffrey

If I were asked to choose which influence was the most important in my life, I'd have to answer that it was my parents. Neither fit the patterns of style and behavior in the 1920s, '30s, and '40s for our middle-class status.

During the Depression, our family was better off than many in Upper Montclair, New Jersey, where we resided while my father commuted to his job in downtown Manhattan as research director for the Chamber of Commerce and Industry. We were more secure financially because my mother had a premonition of disaster in the summer of 1929 and ceased her stock-market playing, insisting that my father do so also. Consequently, there was that little extra money available during the worst years of the Depression.

My dad was a Harvard graduate with an M.A. in city planning and management; in 1938, he received his doctorate. He also maintained his Reserve Army status as an Infantry lieutenant colonel, departing every summer to Camp Dix in the New Jersey hinterlands to do war games. I distinctly remember tactical maps spread out on the old deal table in his bedroom, along with his stamp albums. He trained all three of his children—I was the only girl—in close-order drills, and taught us how to run properly, a skill I have found nearly as useful as my older brother did when he was romping through the jungles of Cambodia and Laos.

My mother, whose family had not been able to put her through college, took courses at our local teachers' college, studying, among other exotic subjects, Russian. She nursed my younger brother, Kevin, through seven years of osteomyelitis to health, with a little help from the innovation of penicillin. Then she became a real-estate agent and supported herself admirably after my father's death in 1954. When she earned enough money to do so, she would take a world cruise. She did that five times.

During World War II, with my father and older brother overseas and Kevin in and out of hospitals and surgery, she coped brilliantly while other women we knew wrung their hands and wept that they were so alone. Nor did Mother complain that she didn't see her husband for five years. Or when, home from a stunning career as a military governor, my father chucked in his safe job in the Chamber of Commerce and Industry, and, disregarding his physical disabilities (he had a history of heart trouble by then, as well as diabetes), went to Japan to restructure their tax system. When the Korean War erupted, Mother did not deny him the right to serve the United Nations Forces as chief finance officer, although that post resulted in the final blow to his health, tuberculosis. He died six months later in a veteran's hospital.

Is it any wonder I write about strong women? From very early on, I was expected to achieve at a high level, constantly exhorted to do so. More subtly, I was indoctrinated with "Well, Anne, you're going to marry and have children and then what are you going to do with the rest of your life?"

With such unorthodox parents, achieving in so many different occupations, I certainly had spectacular role models and was well conditioned to achieve. In fact, it never once occurred to me, during the restrictive years of childbearing, that I did not have the right to do so. I don't think any of us considered that it would be science fiction that I would be doing for the rest of my life. But I certainly don't complain.

There again, parental influence dominated. We were read to as children, my father declaiming Longfellow and Kipling's poems; Mother narrating the *Just-So Stories* and Mowgli, and offering me A. Merritt's *Ship Of Ishtar*. My early conditioning to science fiction and fantasy undoubtedly sprang from those days.

Helpful, too, was the fact that I was such an opinionated, asocial, extroverted, impossible, egregious brat that I was forced to books as companions; none of the children my age would play with me. I developed a tendency to talk with the family cats and, later, when Dad got me riding lessons at the South Orange Armory, horses. I was horse-hooked by the time I was nine. In my loneliness, I used to challenge myself to do great deeds and achieve impossible goals. I'd make them sorry they wouldn't play with me; they'd be sorry they'd ignored me and teased me. I'd be rich and famous. I think I had in mind the ever-alluring notion of a screen career, as I was already "acting" to get attention. My size, rather plain countenance (I've improved with the years as good wine does), and gift for acting led me more to character parts than the leads I would have preferred. Though I trained as a dramatic soprano and had both volume and range, like Killashandra, there was an unattractive burr in my voice, which was useful for singing character parts but unpleasant for Aïda, for instance, or Princess Turandot. More suitable for the Old Lady in Bernstein's original *Candide*, or an old witch in Carl Orff's Christmas pageant, or Queen Aggravaine in *Once Upon a Mattress*, Margot the Innkeeper in *The Vagabond King*, and the Medium in Gian Carlo Menotti's opera—or singing descant above full choir and organ in the Presbyterian Church in Wilmington, Delaware.

The early lessons I learned, generally the hard way, in standing up for myself and my egocentricities, being proud of being "different," doing my own thing, gave me the strength of purpose to continue doing so in later life. You have to learn how not to conform, how to avoid labels. But it isn't easy! It's lonely until you realize that you have inner resources that those of the herd mentality cannot enjoy. That's where the mind learns the freedom to think science-fictiony things, and where early lessons of tenacity, pure bullheadedness, can make a difference. Most people prefer to be accepted. I learned not to be. I also learned that I had a right to marriage, children, and a later-life career. (Mind you, I lost the husband after twenty years, but as his second wife also divorced him, perhaps the faults were not all on my independent head.)

I wouldn't, in the ordinary way, have done such an analysis of influence and effect, but lately Anne McCaffrey has been the subject of three doctoral dissertations, ten masters' theses, and innumerable book reports. Questions have been posed that required a certain amount of introspection on my part. One doctoral candidate proposed that I used the Cinderella legend in all my stories. I fear I took strong exception to this theory. Cinderella was a wimp: none of my heroines are the least bit tinged with that character fault. Other flaws, yes, but not passive resistance.

In point of fact, my first heroine, Sara of *Restoree*, was created as an anodyne to the then-common depiction of females in science fiction: the convenient "idiot" for whom the "science" of the yarn must be explained; the adjunct to prove that the hero was all male; the stupid wimp who stood in a corner, shrieking and wringing her hands while her hero was being mangled by some E.T. menace, animate or inanimate. No way would I have been standing in any corner, weeping or inactive. I've had my share of bruises from contact sports or menace, and scars on my arms to prove I was brave/stupid enough to part the jaws of warring canines. This lack of valid characterization in science fiction incensed me, and I know that it prevented the field from attracting many female readers. Which suited the male dominated readership for a long time, until the less romantic wars and the presence of a female following began to require valid portrayals of all the personae dramatis in a science fiction/fantasy story.

Nevertheless, it was "Star Trek" and later *Star Wars* that broadened the base of readership for the entire field. Indeed, many of my women readers have admitted that they turned to science fiction when they could no longer get a fresh "hit" of "Star Trek" in the 1960s.

Generally speaking, I don't "do" messages in my novels (except for *Decision at Doona*, written during the Vietnam War, wherein my male protagonist remarks, "Mankind will be mature as a species when it no longer feels the need to impose its moral judgments on anybody or anything"). What I do do is practice what I preach and write what I practice. The example is there in the action of the stories, and the effect that the stories have unexpectedly wrought on their readers remains one of the most heartening aspects of being a writer.

The Ship Who Sang, for instance, is much appreciated by the handicapped, who see in Helva the chance to surmount their physical problems and *be* a spaceship. The Harper Hall series has turned more young people on to reading than any of the adult-chosen "recommended" reading lists. Everyone would love to own a dragon of Pern, for that touches on a universal wish to be understood, to be not alone, as well as to be able to travel instantaneously anywhere.

My best advice to aspiring writers, though, is to believe what you are writing so completely that you as the writer participate in the actions/emotions. There

◆ *Anne McCaffrey*

is a curious alchemy that, despite the many processes
to which manuscripts are subjected in the course of
being published, allows the action/emotion to be trans-
lated as experienced to the reader.

In a brief phrase: tell me a story, show me a vision,
and believe it yourself! I do!

Biographical Notes

Born in Cambridge, Massachusetts, Anne McCaffrey returned there to study Slavonic languages and literature, earn-
ing a B.A. degree *cum laude* from Radcliffe College. After
working as an advertising copywriter for Liberty Music Shops
and then Helena Rubinstein, she married Wright Johnson,
had three children, and directed opera and operetta on a free-
lance basis, occasionally performing in shows herself.

Ms. McCaffrey published her first short story in 1954 but
did not publish with regularity until the 1960s, when the
Helva stories began to attract attention. She began to write
full time in 1965, and from 1968 to 1970, served as secretary-
treasurer of the Science Fiction Writers of America. To date,
she has published over thirty-five stories, twelve novels, a
collection of short stories, an anthology, and a cookbook.
Weyr Search won her the Hugo award in 1967, and *Dragon-
rider* (also from the Harper Hall series) claimed the Nebula
award in 1968, making her the first woman to win both
awards. She has lectured at universities, high schools, and

library study groups in the United States, has been an honored guest at numerous conventions, and has appeared on television and radio on both sides of the Atlantic. Since her divorce in 1970, she has lived in Ireland with her children.

Books by Anne McCaffrey

The Lady (Ballantine, 1987)

Nerilka's Story (Ballantine, 1986)

The Girl Who Heard Dragons (Cheap Street, 1986)

The Year of the Lucy (Brandywyne Books, 1985)

Killashandra (Ballantine/Del Rey, 1984)

Stitch in Snow (Underwood-Miller, 1984)

Dinosaur Planet Survivors (Ballantine/Del Rey, 1984)

The Coelura (Underwood-Miller, 1983)

Moreta: Dragonlady of Pern (Ballantine/Del Rey, 1983)

Crystal Singer (Ballantine/Del Rey, 1982)

The Dragonriders of Pern (Ballantine, 1979)

Dragondrums (Atheneum Publishers and Bantam Books, 1979)

The White Dragon (Ballantine, 1978)

Dinosaur Planet (Ballantine, 1978)

Get off the Unicorn (Ballantine, 1977)

Dragonsinger (Atheneum Publishers and Bantam Books, 1977)

Dragonsong (Atheneum Publishers and Bantam Books, 1976)

◆ *Anne McCaffrey*

A Time When (NESFA, 1975)

Kilternan Legacy (Dell, 1975)

Cooking out of this World (Ballantine, 1973)

To Ride Pegasus (Ballantine, 1973)

The Mark of Merlin (Dell, 1971)

Dragonquest (Ballantine, 1971)

Ring of Fear (Dell, 1971)

The Ship Who Sang (Ballantine Books and Walker and Company, 1970)

Alchemy & Academe (Doubleday, 1970)

Decision at Doona (Ballantine, 1969)

Dragonflight (Ballantine Books and Walker and Company, 1968)

Restoree (Ballantine, 1967)

QUESTIONS, QUESTIONS

Patricia C. Hodgell

Y ou ask me why I write. For as long as I can remember, I've always wanted to. My childhood had a lot to do with that. I grew up in an old house full of old books, in a neighborhood full of old people. In fact, my grandmother raised me. She also read aloud to me a great deal, which gave me a strong, early taste for literature. By the time I could read for myself, I much preferred books to the few children who had begun to infiltrate the neighborhood as the old folk died off.

Not surprisingly, given the above, I began to live largely in fantasy worlds, which were at first always someone else's. I devoured things like Tarzan, Doc Savage, Tom Swift (*pere et fils*), and especially superhero comic books, which were just coming into their own at the time. It was mostly second- or third-rate literature at best, but it triggered frequent, intense bursts of enthusiasm in me that blotted out nearly everything else for days at a time. When that happened, I moved into that other world, or rather I should say my alter ego did. I've always found Thurber's Walter Mitty extremely embarrassing. To put oneself into a fantasy has always struck me as very dangerous and rather pathetic, like an admission that one can't deal with the world as it is. I got around this inhibition by creating an alter ego, who drew many of her character traits from me but from whom I still maintained a certain distance. A bit of self-deception, of course, but it worked . . .

. . . most of the time. I do remember a day when I was in the seventh or eighth grade, when I decided that it all had to stop. Growing up Methodist does not encourage such self-indulgence, nor do poor grades from teachers who repeatedly catch one daydreaming in class. So I tried not to fantasize. For one whole day. It was awful, like being half-dead. I never seriously tried to give up fantasy again.

Then came high school. My grandmother died, so I had to move to a different town, away from my beloved house with all its books. I was a prof's kid in this new community because my mother was an associate professor at the local university. That gave me a ready-made social circle of other profs' kids, but somehow I still didn't fit in. None of us was particularly happy. Typical acts of rebellion for the others consisted of smoking pot, burning draft cards (this being the Vietnam era), and climbing the water tower. Just to be perverse, I took up studying. At about the same time,

I discovered Tolkien and nineteenth-century literature, both of which came as something of a shock to someone raised on the Shadow, Batman, and Zorro.

My own fantasy world developed slowly. Until I learned how to concentrate in high school, there really wasn't much of it that wasn't heavily derivative and pretty thinly conceived at that. More and more, though, I found myself edging out of other people's stories and into the hinterlands of my own. Not that I was writing much of it down yet—just story fragments and plot ideas, furiously melodramatic, violent stuff, mostly, as my more idle daydreams still tend to be. Still, some themes and characters were beginning to emerge that have stuck with me ever since. And I also began trying to visualize scenes. Apparently I'd never done that before, because that first, carefully built-up image is still clear in my mind, as flat and static as ever, like a comic-book panel by a not particularly good artist.

Things didn't really begin to move until I started to write seriously. That wasn't until college. Why did it take me so long to get it out? Probably because, as badly as I wanted to be a writer, I was even more afraid of being a failure. In some ways, to think of myself *as* a writer was for me the ultimate Walter Mitty fantasy. But I also had a sense that time was running out. Either I had to prove to myself that I could write, or it was high time that I figured out something else to do with my life. So I took a year off after college and went back to the old house, determined to try.

That year produced only two or three stories, notably the first draft of "Stranger Blood." At the end of it came the Clarion Writers' Workshop. I really had no idea what I was getting into. My only previous contact with the science-fiction world had been a visit to my college by Kate Wilhelm, Damon Knight, and Piers Anthony. I had asked them what advice they had for someone who wanted to write. Anthony (who at that time had just finally made enough money to buy an electric typewriter) said, "Don't even try." Kate said, "Go to Clarion."

The workshop provided two major shocks. The first was finding out that I really could write after all—well enough, in fact, to sell to Kate and to Harlan Ellison, who bought my first and second stories. The other surprise was discovering a whole community of other people like me, who also dreamed. I suppose that was also the first time it sank in that what I was doing and wanted to do was actually acceptable behavior—not just a retreat from reality, as I had always feared, but the creation of new realities, each one with the potential power to thrill readers as much as other writers' work had thrilled me. At last, I had a justification for the self-absorbed way I had grown up, for all the day-dreams and my continued indulgence in them. In short, Clarion was the turning point of my life.

You ask me why I write what I do. Couldn't the themes I deal with be handled just as well in mainstream fiction?

They probably could, and often have been, very well indeed, by other writers. But I simply couldn't deal with them that way. I wouldn't know how. My imagination is apparently trained to think only in fantasy terms, at least when it comes to storytelling. I can imagine real-life scenarios for myself (although very rarely and almost with embarrassment, which probably explains why I have a better idea of my characters' futures than of my own); but if I'm writing fiction, it apparently has to be fantasy.

Perhaps, in my case, it would make more sense to consider why I'm committed to telling this particular story. As it turns out, I'm not the usual, versatile fantasist. With one brief exception (*Last Dangerous Visions*, written overnight as a Clarion assignment and bought by Harlan Ellison), all my fiction, short and long, is part of the same story. I seem to have latched onto something huge, off of which I keep chipping bits. I don't know how many pieces will ultimately make up the whole. I don't even know for certain what the whole is. I certainly didn't plan to land in this position, holding the tail of such a tiger.

Apparently, it's very important to me to tell this particular story, about how my alter ego, Jame, finds a place in her world. I've come to realize that, on one level, this is almost a fantasy autobiography. Lots of very personal elements have crept in. For example, consider Jame's father. He kicks her out of the house as a child. He curses her. He is apparently a complete bastard. She finds a much more acceptable father figure in the Kendar Marc, who is (it seems to me) pretty much everything one could want in a parent. I simply wrote about these two men. It took a friend to point out to me that I had split my own father into two people: the one who ran out of the hospital when he heard that he had a daughter instead of a son, who divorced my mother when I was two; and the one whom I came to know as I grew up, who was as kind and

33

generous as any child could wish. When I sent him a copy of my first novel, he wrote back that while I had set out to create fantasy, I had described reality instead. I still haven't had the nerve to ask him exactly what he meant by that.

Another theme that figures strongly in *Dark of the Moon* is that of the missing or dead sibling. I had a baby brother who died before I was born, but he was still part of my childhood because I knew that the little box containing his ashes was in the back of the handkerchief drawer. He was my brother-in-the-box, gone but not departed. He's still there, under the photograph of a luckless uncle who, during World War II, first walked off a battleship and then accidentally shot himself in the head with his own rifle. The sea will give up its dead before this old house does.

All of this rather highlights my situation. I seem to write fantasy as a way of bringing real life—*my* life— into perspective and of coping with it. I guess that makes me my own ideal audience, although, from the letters I get, it appears that some readers react to this fiction as strongly as I do, and in much the same way. Interestingly enough, these people usually appear to be about my own age, not the children or young adults for whom my work is primarily marketed. I never meant to be a children's writer. That was accidental, a marketing fluke—unless, perhaps, such literature appeals to anyone, of whatever age, who still feels shy of maturity. God knows, I frequently do myself. Perhaps that's what I'm seeking. I do know that I feel compelled first to create a world as a writer and then explore it as a character. The world seems to come largely from my subconscious mind. I'm seldom entirely sure what's happening in my mind's more dynamic bits, which have an unnerving habit of simply springing out at me from the undergrowth. Then my conscious mind, in the guise of my heroine, has to find out exactly what's going on. In her world, everything depends on her getting it right. In mine too, maybe.

Not that I set out with any such didactic goal, nor do I feel obliged to hammer away at it as I work. Primarily, I write to entertain. It's just that I find it more and more important that my heroine make the right decisions, for the right reasons—and I'm not making it easy for her. What the hell. Is it easy for any of us to separate right from wrong (or even right from left, if you're as directionally dyslexic as I am)? Then, too, the more risks, the more thrills. After all, it was that element of excitement that first drew me to literature, long before I thought to look for good characterization, competent writing, or even correct grammar. God forbid I should ever sacrifice good story values to messages of any sort but, then again, why shouldn't I? The two aren't mutually exclusive. In fact, I generally enjoy a story more if it has some serious purpose under all the swashbuckling. As for my own work, I know only that whatever Jame achieves, against whatever odds, she has to do it honestly, the hard way, because only then will she also be achieving something important for me and, I hope, for any reader who comes adventuring with us.

You ask me what effect it's had on this whole process that I happen to be a woman.

Not a lot, I think.

It was, of course, a great advantage to come into the field in the wake of someone like Le Guin and just slightly behind such fine writers as McKinley and McKillip. If there ever was any prejudice against female fantasists, these people pretty well destroyed it.

On the other hand, readers apparently don't always realize that I'm a woman. In fact, booksellers tell me that most customers assume I'm male, until told differently. On top of that, I've repeatedly been "praised" by reviewers for my masculine style or even, heaven help me, for my "masculine verbs." Robin McKinley tells me that she's had the same problem. There seems to be a perception loose in the land that clear, direct prose (which I would simply characterize as "good") is somehow exclusively masculine. What, then, is a female writing style? Unclear, indirect—bad? How idiotic.

It strikes me, though, that readers also identify a certain type of writing with male authors. The popular conception seems to be that men write action-oriented stories while women concentrate more on romance. Take, for example, all the men who write gothic romances under female noms de plume, and the no less uncommon number of women who write adventure stories using their initials or under male aliases. In our field, does this boil down to a perception that men write science fiction and women write fantasy? I'm not sure. Epic fantasy or sword-and-sorcery tales seem to be popularly conceived as in the male sphere of dominance, if readers' reactions to my own work are any indication, perhaps because both of these subgenres are primarily action oriented. Personally, I try to ignore any distinction or sexual stereotype that limits the choices of women *or* men.

That's probably one reason I use my initials. This practice would seem to link me to women writers of the past who have used such means to hide their sex, which is why Kate Wilhelm tried very hard to talk me out of it when I first started out. So why did I insist on ambiguity? Probably because "P. C. Hodgell" was what I wrote on my dormitory door at Clarion. I had never used the initials before. I did so then without thinking, and suddenly it was as if I had created a whole new persona. Pat Hodgell had dreamed of being a writer for most of her life, but a terror of failure had kept her from even putting pen to paper. Meanwhile, Patricia C. Hodgell had developed a taste for academics which led her to a doctorate in English literature. But P. C. Hodgell, the writer, might be able to realize the dearest fantasy of both. Creative schizophrenia. Whatever gets you through. I found that I couldn't give up the sense of freedom that the initials gave me, even though I knew I was likely to be criticized for them. Anyway, I was going into a field already rife with such names as C. S. Lewis, E. R. Eddison, H. P. Lovecraft and, of course, J.R.R. Tolkien. Ultimately, I didn't see why I should have to give up a convention that all of these men found so useful, just because I was a woman.

You ask me what part feminism plays in my writing. From the above, one might assume that it doesn't have much of a role at all but that's not true. Here again, we touch on a subject with roots in my childhood. I grew up in a house occupied, off and on, by three generations of women and no males at all, except for the occasional tomcat and, of course, my dead brother. The impression I got, growing up, was that it really wasn't necessary to have men around at all, at least not on a daily basis. We coped quite well on our own. Women should cope, I thought, just as in general they should accept responsibilities for their own lives and ask no favors. It was a sort of unconscious feminism, a sense of how things should be, even if they sometimes fell short. I still cringe a bit when I have to call in a workman for a job that I think I should be able to do myself, but even the most ardent feminist might be daunted by a spouting water heater or a spark-spitting electrical outlet.

I see the same attitude in Jame—not surprisingly, I suppose, since she *is* my alter ego. She doesn't think in terms of what women should or shouldn't do, and she doesn't wait for others to do things for her. She simply decides what needs to be done and does it, to the best of her ability, and then copes with the often disastrous consequences. I admire her independence and resourcefulness tremendously. She seems to me to be the ideal feminist; that is, one who takes her equality for granted and goes on from there. She's going to be in for a shock, though, when she finds out how her own people expect her to behave.

I have noticed one odd thing about her, though: she seems to be becoming increasingly, even unnervingly, androgynous. Throughout *God Stalk*, most of Tai-tastigon assumed she was a boy, despite her best efforts to disillusion everyone. In *Dark of the Moon*, she was repeatedly mistaken for her twin brother, Torisen. In the as yet untitled (and unwritten) third novel, she becomes Tori's heir, which allows her to be treated as a male, *and* a hill chief adopts her as his youngest son, much to her confusion. She courts none of this. It simply happens, despite her protests. Neither of us knows exactly what's going on here, and both of us are very puzzled by it.

I do note, however, that all of this has to do almost exclusively with how others perceive Jame, not with how she sees herself. And it relates to changes in her social status. In her world, there really aren't many options for a woman of her race and class. In order to escape the social strictures, she has to take advantage of any loopholes she can find and, as usual, cope with the consequences as they come.

What it all comes down to, I think, is that I'm really more interested in developing a character as an individual rather than as a male or female, just as P.C. is far more concerned with becoming a good writer than with projecting either a male or female persona. I never think, "How can I make this particular character more masculine or feminine?" (Does anyone? That sounds to me like a recipe for disaster.) Rather, I ask, "Who is this person? Where does s/he come from? What is s/he like?" or, occasionally, "Is this someone who I am going to shape to fit a certain, preconceived part, or is s/he going to shape the plot by her/his evolving character?"

Characters who shape the plot are the really interesting ones to me, even if they do sometimes make hash of my carefully planned storyline. I find that, most often, they are also the alienated members of their society, the outsiders who still want—oh, so badly—to belong in some way. To me, they are "the other," female or male, who are also my distorted mirror images. Jame is the most obvious one, the truest reflection. Her people would like to regard her as totally alien—in fact, as some sort of demonic changeling to be rejected and destroyed. That would be the simple solution. What they really fear is that strange as Jame is, she might turn out to be human after all, and therefore not be something that they can simply reject out of hand. What they haven't realized yet is that not only Jame's future but their own depends on their ability to accept her—strangeness, frightening potential, and all.

But there are male "aliens," too. Bane is a good example. I originally created him to fill a minor niche in *God Stalk* as a more or less two-dimensional bully, but he kept filling out. First I discovered that he was half-Kencyr, and then that he was Jame's half-brother. I don't know exactly what he is now. We last saw him presumably being stabbed to death by a Tasitigon mob, but I've since caught a glimpse of him, or at least of something rather like a cross between him and the Lower Town Monster (the demon created with his stolen soul) in the high passes of the Ebonbane, crawling westward toward the Riverland. If he ever gets there, Jame will have much the same difficulty with him that the rest of the Kencyrath has with her: if he is purely demonic now, she needn't hesitate to destroy him if she can; but if, somehow, he is still at least part human, then she's got a problem. If I understand the challenge of "the other" correctly, it is that, ultimately, there is no such thing.

Finally, you ask me in what direction I see my work heading. For the foreseeable future, it will probably forge straight ahead. This is, after all, a very long, complex story I'm trying to work out and, as I said, it's very important to me to get it right. I've certainly set myself enough puzzles to keep me out of trouble and Jame in it for years to come. After that, who knows? In the meantime, I will continue to work out Jame's story, looking in it for the signposts that so often mark my own life.

Biographical Notes

Patricia C. Hodgell was born in Des Moines, Iowa and was raised in Oshkosh, Wisconsin. Patricia received an undergraduate degree in comparative literature from Eckerd College in Florida. Ms. Hodgell continued her graduate studies at the University of Minnesota, obtaining both an M.A. and a Ph.D. in English. Patricia currently teaches at the University of Wisconsin in Oshkosh and is a lecturer for the University of Minnesota's Independent Study program.

Ms. Hodgell's novel, *Dark of the Moon*, was named best novel by the Conclave of Wisconsin Writers in 1985. She has been the Guest of Honor at Novacon 9 science fiction convention. Patricia currently resides in her ancestral home in Oshkosh, Wisconsin with her two Siamese cats and is completing the third novel in the *God Stalk* trilogy.

Books by P. C. Hodgell

Dark of the Moon (Atheneum, 1985)
God Stalk (Atheneum, 1982)

◆

A Woman Writing Science Fiction and Fantasy

Alice Sheldon

f you squeeze a mouse, it squeaks.

Just so, when life squeezes me, I squeak. That is, I write. And from my middle years I have felt squeezed by life. First there is the sky-darkening presence of the patriarchy, the male-run society, all about me and over me, cutting off my options. And then there is the physical crowding. It is increasingly impossible to get away from other people's noise, smells, bodies; their radios, the ringing of my phone by strangers, strangers' houses springing up everywhere in what had been lovely countryside; strangers' cars crowding the roads twenty-four hours a day; strangers' garbage polluting my aquifers, other people's junk polluting the world; footprints and tire tracks on every patch of new-fallen snow, chain saws and bulldozers in every patch of woodland; hostile strangers menacing me if I walk out of my house by night or day. And no end in sight. Unless our birthrate falls drastically, we are on our way to being another Bangladesh.

So much for my personal squeezedness.

But beyond that I am wounded, revolted by what man is doing to the planet. I love the natural earth. The space photos that show our wonderful green-and-blue world floating lonely in black space have driven home its fragility. Remember those photos? Remember the great ugly red-brown scars of deserts on them? Those deserts are growing, the green is shrinking. And the blue, our sacred blue oceans, are being defiled by the dumping of everything from sewage and tar to radioactive wastes. Even the Sargasso Sea, that remote breeding place of species, is now poisoned with biphenylated plastics. The great rich rain forests are being burned and felled at an appalling rate. The very top of Mount Everest has garbage on it. Species after species of Earth's wonderful creation are becoming extinct as I write this. We have already killed half of the Northeast of our continent with acid rain, and dumped enough CO_2 into our air to change the climate for the worse. I weep for earth.

And then, not least, there is what man is doing to man—and woman. His endless wars, his compulsion to competition and aggression and dominance appalls me. About forty wars are raging right now, and we all live under the shadow of his grandest war, which will end us and take the planet's life with it. Greed rules our daily intercourse: the rich and powerful grab everything in sight. Those who should be our leaders flaunt their corruption, while the poor get poorer and turn to violent crime to assuage their wants. Where cooperation is so sorely needed, we live in a war of all against all.

And, with the frontiers gone, it is a zero-sum gain. The winners win always at others' expense. Who will civilize us?

Most personal to me is the plight of women. They are at the bottom of every class heap, struggling in a world that has no place for humane values, condemned to do the hard, unpaid chores of the world. Vivid in my memory is a small band of tribal women, who each day walked for water three miles over violently rocky hillsides, returning with five-gallon, forty-pound loads balanced on their heads—and doing this, for the most part, with one baby on their backs and another in their bellies. They were not praised nor paid for this—it was "women's work." In our land of "opportunity," their physical work is less, but the stress is greater. No wonder that the poorest of the poor turn, as children, to having unneeded babies simply to garner a little love.

And things will not grow better. If trouble comes to our system, as come I fear it will, it will be liberation of women that is blamed for it. Our "rights" will vanish like snow in summer as the stronger, agressive animals we live among vent their frustration.

Nor will time improve things. In a world where the raising of children yields no profit (except to television salesmen) the young are left to raise themselves, in the dumb, time-wasting enclaves of the schools and the culture of the streets and of television. When they become the adults, how will they rule?

And I have another, private pain. I love the English language, that noble mongrel. It is my aim to speak and write it clearly and colorfully. But daily I must listen to insipid gibberish from the mouths of our so-called leaders. How can we think clearly if our minds are stuffed with rubbishy slogans?

For all these reasons, then, I write. My first serious story showed a man so driven to despair that he spread a mortal disease in order to save the earth. And in nearly all of my seventy-plus stories since, one or more of my distresses forms the undertheme. So much for my deeper motivation.

But this list of agonies could as well have inspired articles, diatribes like Jeremiah's. Why write stories? Ah, therein lies the mystery. I do not think we will know the answer until we know why the first caveman lifted his voice and regaled his fellows with a made-up tale. True, he might have been rewarded with an extra knucklebone to chew, as Scheherazade was rewarded with an extra day of life for each chapter she recounted. But that does not explain it. The urge to make stories is inbuilt, primeval.

Well, then, why write science fiction? I could say because I have always read it, since I discovered *Weird Tales* at the age of nine. So when I came to write a story, it seemed natural to send it off to *Analog*. But the fact is that I have a modest view of my talent. I haven't the ear for rhythm or the feel for style to encourage me to compete in the serious mainstream. And I certainly haven't the stomach to write mainstream schlock, like *Jaws* or *Gone With The Wind*. Science fiction suits me just right. Science fiction is the literature of ideas, and I am, I think, an idea writer. Science fiction allows extrapolation into the future, and that is my natural way of thought. ("If this goes on . . . ,") And science fiction is the literature of wonder: you have only to say, "Those lights in the sky are great suns" for me to go all shivery. In science fiction I have found my niche.

Will science fiction and fantasy continue? Yes, I think, but perhaps they may suffer a certain decline. In the last fifty years we have burned up ideas at a breakneck rate and, while the stock of ideas surely is not finite, the new ones may not come along as fast as we could hope. Of course, there is always cinema; the movies now are using the ideas that were done in the literature thirty years ago, and the public may slowly adapt so it can use the newer ones. As to fantasy, I don't know. Who could have predicted Tolkien? I'm not primarily a fantasy writer, so I don't know how fast the ideas there are being used up. In any event, I doubt the public will continue to read much except comic books.

Are there things you can say in science fiction that you can't say in mainstream? Well, no, I think; not really. But if you were writing up a given idea for the mainstream, you would have to go to the endless bother of introducing it and soothing incredulity and generally tempering the wind to the shorn lamb—whereas in

science fiction you can just start in, and your readers
know at once that it's After the Atom Bombs Fall or
whatever.

Which brings up the Ideal Reader. For whom do I
write? I honestly don't know. I used to think I wrote
for bright young minds who might say, "Well, I never
thought of that before!" And, of course, I write to sat-
isfy myself. No one pressures me, since I do not write
to eat. But, judging from my fan mail, there is simply
no common denominator among my readers, beyond
the fact that they seem literate. I suspect I write at
heart for people like myself, souls who love and fear
what I do. And I suspect a majority of them are women,
though my mail is predominantly from the other sex.

As to the question of whether there are male and
female writing styles, here I may part company from
other women. I feel that by their sins shall ye know
them, which is to say that there are separate styles in
bad writing. Rebecca West has said that the sin of men
is lunacy and the sin of women idiocy. She meant that
men have the weakness of seeing everything in black
and white, as though by moonlight, with all the colors
and pains left out, like a shiny new machine. And "idiocy" derives from the original meaning of "idiot," a
private person. Women can be over-obsessed by min-
utiae, by trivial concerns with no broad implications.
This is only natural in a gender evolved to rear children;* raising the young is a matter of endless minu-

---

*Please notice that I said women are evolved to rear children, *not* to enjoy
it or find it totally fulfilling. To say that they are not so evolved is to fly
in the face of all we see in other primates. And watch any pair of parents
with a newborn baby. It is the mother who is in her element.

tiae, which are big concerns for the growing child. When women write badly, they fall away from the larger human concerns into too-private trivialisms. When men write badly, it is about some sublunar crackpot idea with no regard for its real human consequences—like their wars.

I think there is a general human way of writing, of telling tales of challenge and response, of trials and strivings—and, in science fiction, of wondrous alien systems that can illuminate our own. Men and women deviate from this central style according to their experience and inclinations, but there is not much difference. It may be that men have the edge slightly in black humor, and women in heart-wringing, but that is certainly cultural.

I see that I omitted one masculine style of writing that particularly bores and irritates me: that is the ineffable tale of boy-becomes—surprise!—a-MAN. This is a story, if you can call it such, peculiar to the patriarchy. No woman so relishes, today, the grand elevation to adult status. Maybe we should; certainly to be a woman—if self-defined, not defined by men—is no mean achievement. But it carries with it too many problems to simply be greeted with hosannahs.

I see here the interesting question about whether it is man or woman who can be seen as the alien, the Other. Yet it seems obvious: from my viewpoint, it is the male who is the alien. It is understandable that women could view themselves as alien to male society—a viewpoint of despair, I think. But if you take what you are as the normal human, as any self-respecting person is bound to do, then it is clear that to a woman writer, men are very abnormal indeed, most men anyway. We understand them better than they understand us, in the same way that the subordinates in any group understand the dominant ones better than the dominators understand them. (A source of agony to many bosses, who assume that the darkies are happy singing minstrels and then are caught short by bloody revolution.) And we understand men better because, if I may be chauvinistic, understanding is our business. We can't get on without it, as a man can.

And I have used the idea of man-as-alien in my story, "The Women Men Don't See," in which a pair of women decide to go and live with some real aliens after lifetimes of coping with the aliens around them.

Perhaps this answers the question of what role feminism plays in the content of my work. But to answer it more fully, I have to recount a bit of personal history.

I came into the field of science fiction as a man— that is, under a male pseudonym, which I stuck to so completely that even my agent, Bob Mills, believed I was male. There was an initial reason for using it; two reasons, rather. The first was that I wanted to conceal my writing from my colleagues in the university. (I am a retired experimental psychologist.) I was already known as an adherent of what were then regarded as weird ethological theories, my colleagues being strict Hullsians, and the news that I wrote science fiction would have been the crowning blow to my respectability. Second—and mainly—I was sure the first stories wouldn't sell. I was prepared to spend the traditional five years papering the walls with rejection slips. So I

chose what seemed an innocuous name off a marma-
lade jar in the Giant supermarket and added a "Junior"
to it for confusion's sake. I intended to try a different
name with each submission, so the editors wouldn't
associate me with all those rejects.

But then the first two stories sold—and the next,
and the next, and I was stuck with "Tiptree, James Jr."
I thought this was a good joke, and greatly enjoyed my
anonymity. (I am a reclusive type, afraid of meeting
people, except on paper.) I went on happily writing
stories, all of which, to my amazement, continued to
sell—and I was quite unaware of the curiosity I was
provoking in the science-fiction community. (A squad
of fans once actually staked out my McLean, Virginia,
post-office box when the big science-fiction convention
was in D.C.—luckily I was in Canada at the time.)
Quite a few pages were written elucidating who and
what I must be and, while a certain number of obser-
vant souls deduced that I must be a woman, nobody
really knew, and others were as positive that I was
male.

The stories I wrote then were just about the same
as I write today, with one exception: a few violently
pro-woman ideas came to me, and I saw that they were
simply not credible under a man's name, so I invented
a female pseudonym (Raccoona Sheldon) for these. Raccoona lived in Wisconsin and her mail was a terrible
headache to the local postmistress—and me.

During that decade of being James, I corresponded
freely with all sorts of science-fiction people, princi-
pally as a result of my habit of writing fan letters to

writers I admired. And I made what I thought were good friends. Though I didn't reveal my true names, I always told the plain truth about myself in my letters; my biography is ambi-sexual—Army, government, academe—and offered no real clue to my gender or identity. I also told a few close friends about my trials with my aged, widowed mother, then living, or rather dying, in Chicago, and that she had been an African explorer and writer. So when Mary did die, in 1977, one of these friends saw the newspaper obituaries and my secret was out.

Oddly enough, that shattered me. I felt I could never write again. My secret world had been invaded and the attractive figure of Tiptree—he *did* strike several people as attractive—was revealed as nothing but an old lady in Virginia. No more speculations about my "mysterious" travels, or that I might be the secret spy master of the CIA. Worse, I was no longer able to be my female correspondents' "understanding" male friend, or say things to editors like "Why aren't there any women writers in this anthology?" Now I was just another woman with my own tale of woes. No magic. And I stood ashamed before the women writers who had used their own female names in cracking the predominantly male world of science fiction. I had taken the easy path.

But *was* it easier, getting accepted as a man? I can't honestly tell, except by indirection. You see, after the revelation, quite a few male writers who had been, I thought, my friends and called themselves my admirers, suddenly found it necessary to adopt a condescending, patronizing tone, or break off our correspondence altogether, as if I no longer interested them. (I can only conclude that I didn't.) If that is how I would have been received from the start, my hat is off to those brave women writing as women.

And there have been no more Nebulas, except one to Raccoona. No more Hugos. I can't believe that the quality of my stuff has deteriorated so suddenly. Of course, though, it may be that I withdrew too many stories at the last minute. For example, I pulled out *The Women Men Don't See* when it looked like it might win, because I thought too many women were rewarding a man for being so insightful, and that wasn't fair. People may have thought I undervalued the award. So that isn't a clear result of my "sex change." But it *is* depressing, since I personally think one or two of my best have been written since then.

But as I think it over, and think also of the fact that some of the male writers who have been a touch snotty to me seem genuinely friendly to other women writers, I think there is a deeper problem. People dislike being fooled and, quite innocently, I did fool them for ten years. Moreover, it seems to be very important, especially to men, to know the sex of the person they are dealing with. What's the use of being Number One in a field of two—that is, male—if people can't tell the difference? I had not only fooled them, I had robbed them of relative status. . . . Clearly, friendship is out of the question after that.

So, there is my somewhat unconventional history of male/female relations in my work. And I believe it answers certain aspects of other questions, too. Those that remain seem to have to do with writing itself.

As to how I develop a character, I do it the same way we come to know people in life—by telling what they do and listening to what they say. I haven't had occasion to develop any very complicated characters yet, as, for example, a wily hypocrite. I would do this, I imagine, by showing his hypocrisy. He might be driving along in a car, expatiating on his goodheartedness and universal sympathy, and suddenly a child lets his puppy loose in the street ahead. The car hits it, the child screams—and Mr. Benevolent simply accelerates, continuing to talk.

I believe this is how all writers develop character, some more subtly than others. Of course, there is the useful way of doing it fast, by reporting what other characters say or think about him. But that's nothing new.

And as to what kind of writer I think I am, and how I fit in the world of science fiction, I believe I am, as I mentioned, an idea writer with a talent for fleshing out what might be impersonal ideas, like time travel, so that the reader takes them as real.

And I am also, deep down, a teller of cautionary tales. "If this goes on—Look Out!" I sometimes wonder if my readers get the cautionary element, or whether it is buried under too much color and flesh. For instance, one of my Hugo winners was a tale of an alien race that has a set of powerful instinctual drives that are carrying them to disaster. Part of my intent, in addition to telling a good story, was to warn of the dangers of yielding to instinctive behavior, to our own patterns of aggression, for example. But no one, speaking of the story, seems to have drawn this analogy. Such are the pitfalls of setting up your message as the undertheme—although I'd have thought its title, *Love Is the Plan, the Plan Is Death* rather gave things away.

Which concludes all I know of myself as a science fiction writer. I look forward to reading what my sisters will report—doubtless they will say insightful things that open whole new boxes. But I must go back to doing whatever it is we do at the typewriter and keeping faith with the small but devoted band of left-handed penguins whom I see as my readers.

Autobiographical Notes

The first shocks from Mt. Vesuvius struck Pompeii on 24 August AD 70; 1,845 years later on 24 August I started to get bored. In both cases, it would have been better had matters stopped there.

Not that I haven't been fortunate. Lucky? I've been so lucky it nearly killed me. First, I had the luck to be born to a brilliant, lovable, and loving young couple who longed to roam all over then-unknown parts of Africa and Asia for the American Museum of Natural History—and took me with them. The result was that when I was ten, I had walked 2,700 miles through Africa (before radio and planes), had seen my little face on the front pages of newspapers, had been through lots of India and Southeast Asia and Europe, had seen close-range some of the most magnificent lands and miserable humans in the world, and had a case of *horror vitae* that lasted all my life.

But that was only the start. When I was a passable graphics artist, it was my luck that the *New Yorker* magazine owed my mother's agent a favor; later I became a serious (i.e., gold-frame) painter, and Father just happened to be on the Art Institute's Board of Directors when they were looking for Chicago artists; and the same with the Corcoran; when I wanted to be a newspaper writer, Marshall Field, Jr., who owned the *Sun*, was coming to dinner. When the Army Air Force was looking for a presentable WAC in Intelligence to give a big gold-and-pink medal to, my otherwise wonderful husband just happened to be chief honcho in U.S. AAF European Intelligence. And so it went.

By the age of twenty, I was convinced that my only value to the world lay in my being my parents' child or my husband's wife; I myself was nobody and worth nothing. Is it any wonder that when I came to write science fiction, I did it under a false name and slipped the stories, all unagented, into magazines' slush piles, so if they sold I would have *something*, ANYTHING, that I'd done by myself, that rested on the merits of the thing alone?

(I had a piece of natural luck here; I took a man's name just when the big boom in *female* science fiction writers started. To this day, I am omitted from lists of women science fiction writers and, of course, I don't belong in the men's.)

Now, I see I have left out all I was supposed to put in, about working for the CIA and becoming a genuine research psychologist—Ph.D., 1967—which brought me the greatest genuine thrill of my life, and all the rest. But—so it goes.

Biographical Notes

James Tiptree Jr., Raccoona Sheldon, and Alice Sheldon were one and the same person. Alice B. Sheldon was born in Chicago to Mary Hasting Bradley, a journalist and author of travel books. Alice spent much of her childhood in Africa, India, and elsewhere abroad. She did her undergraduate studies at Sarah Lawrence College in New York and received her Ph.D. in experimental psychology from George Washington University. She worked for the C.I.A. and U.S. Army and was involved in psychological research for these agencies.

Alice Sheldon drew from her extensive background in psychology, anthropology, biology, and other sciences to become one of the most influencial science-fiction writers of the 1970s. She arrived at the pseudonym of James Tiptree Jr. when she spied the name on a jam label in the supermarket. Speculation over her true identity raged over the years. It was not until 1977 that her actual identity was revealed, and readers learned that James Tiptree Jr. was a woman. Alice Sheldon won Hugo awards in 1974 and 1979; Nebula awards in 1973, 1976, and 1979; and a *Locus* award in 1984.

In 1987, Alice Sheldon—depressed and despondent over her husband Huntington Sheldon's chronic illness—committed suicide along with him. Her passing was a great loss to the science-fiction community, and she will be missed.

Books by Alice Sheldon

Crown of Stars (Tor Books, 1988)

Starry Rift (Tor Books, 1986)

Tales of the Quintana Roo (Arkham, 1986)

Brightness Falls from the Air (Tor Books, 1985)

Byte Beautiful: Eight Science Fiction Stories (Doubleday, 1985)

Up the Walls of the World (Ace Books, 1984)

Out of Everywhere and Other Extraordinary Visions (Ballantine, 1981)

INTERVIEW

Suzette Haden Elgin

Why do you write?

First, I write because it's a way that I can earn a living and support my family, despite a set of multiple interacting physical handicaps. But I didn't always have those, and even then I wrote, so the financial answer can't be the only one. I think the other answer is that I write in order to explain. People won't, in our culture, sit down and give me enough of their time and attention to make it possible for me to do that in person; even if they would, I couldn't reach very many of them in that way. And so I write.

Why do you write in the genres that you have chosen?

I write in several genres, but I think the one that
interests you is science fiction, so I'll answer the question in that context. I write science fiction because it
offers me several things that are important to me. In
science fiction, I am allowed to include a great deal of
science, in a way that would be allowed in mainstream
fiction only to Great Writers. I can take a scientific
hypothesis and use a science-fiction novel as a forum
to carry out a "thought experiment," to prove or dis-
prove it, when the experiment would be impossible in
the real world. If I wrote mainstream fiction, unless I
were very lucky (or again, a Great Writer), I would be
able to reach only a small number of people . . . perhaps
a thousand is about the maximum. Since I write in
order to explain, a large audience is important to me.
Important enough that if I could write in one of the
fiction categories that has an even larger audience—
romance novels, for example, or gothics—I would do
that like a shot. But I can't; I've tried, and I'm hopeless
at all the other categories.

*What were the obstacles or benefits you encoun-
tered as a woman writing in that genre?*

When I began writing science fiction I didn't know
that being a woman was supposed to cause problems,
or that I should have signed my works "S. H. Elgin"
or any of those things. I didn't know any writers,
knew nothing about the writing business, and just pro-
ceeded to write the work and submit it. It sold, it was
published—no problems. By the time I learned that it

was impossible, I was like the bumblebee; I'd already done it. I am not aware of having had any problems getting published, or getting paid, or anything of that kind, that were due to my being a woman. The problems I've had (vile covers, flap copy that makes it clear the editor has not read the book, things like that) are problems also experienced by all the male science-fiction writers I know. In fact, so far as I know, it is only with my non-fiction that I have encountered obstacles associated with simply being female. There is certainly a problem with the perception of my work; for instance, the short story called "Lest Levitation Come Upon Us," which took me seventeen years to write and is unquestionably the best short story I've ever written—and an absolutely serious story—was described in *Locus* as "a piece of charming silliness by Suzette Haden Elgin." I cannot imagine *Locus* referring to a work by a male writer, no matter how frothy, as "charming silliness." Male "charming silliness"—the *Hitchhiker's Guide to the Galaxy* stuff, for example—is not so described. Finally, if there are any benefits associated with being a woman writing science fiction, I have never encountered them, nor do I know anyone else who has. It's not like the romance genre, where if you're a man you must write under a woman's name. Women writers in science fiction continue to be the underclass, no matter how much men who are having trouble getting published whine and go on about our excessive presence.

Who do you write for? Do you have an "ideal audience"?

I have sometimes written an entire book with the ideal audience being a single real-world individual I just couldn't convince to listen to the explanation in question. Other than that, though, I don't have an ideal audience. Not for fiction. I have a "least ideal" audience, which is that audience composed of Valery's "happy few." I consider it my obligation to be clear, and to be readable without struggle. In nonfiction this gets me called a "popularizer," of course, but not in fiction.

What role does feminism play in your writing?

It plays a major role, more and more all the time. The situation of women keeps getting worse, and so I feel more urgently the need to explain where that is sure to lead. When I first began, in the late 1960s, I wasn't as concerned with feminism because the situation of women was so much better then. But feminism is not my discipline, and I don't know the theory; I am a feminist in the nontechnical sense of the term, and do the best I can.

What sort of future do you see for science fiction and fantasy?

I think it is getting more difficult every day to write science fiction, because things happen so quickly! There was a time when you could imagine some logical extrapolation of the real-world situation and be reasonably sure it would not appear in the real world for at least ten years, giving your book time to appear first and be read first. Not anymore. Now you're lucky if whatever you write about doesn't hit the streets before your book or story does. Fantasy is less at risk. It goes all the way back to the beginnings of recorded history at least, and will surely go all the way forward to the end. Only when something formerly part of fantasy gets "discovered" and is abruptly part of science fiction does it become endangered. (Margaret Atwood's novel *The Handmaid's Tale* is an excellent example of what I mean; ten years ago it would have had to be published as a science-fiction novel, but in today's climate it is accepted as mainstream. That situation will get worse).

What influences and motivates you in your writing?

That's hard to answer, because I'm not sure exactly what you mean. I'll try. I see people in pain—all kinds of pain. Often their pain could be dealt with if something were explained to them, or were explained to those responsible for the pain. I respond to that situation by writing explanations.

How do you view yourself within the science-fiction and fantasy writing community?

As a working-stiff writer. Very small fish. Editors have backed me up in that opinion, many a time; my colleagues have not voted me any awards, nor have my readers, thus confirming my judgment. And that's all right.

What do you find you can say within a science-fiction or fantasy story that couldn't be said in mainstream fiction?

◆ *Suzette Haden Elgin*

I think it's the other way around, if I understand your question correctly. In mainstream fiction you can say literally anything, and people do; my genre is much more conservative. The only thing I know that is close to what you are referring to is the greater tolerance that science-fiction readers have for actual science within their fiction—mainstream readers might refuse to put up with that.

Do you think there is a female writing style? A male style?

No. There's a good deal of research, with conclusions on both sides of the question, but my personal opinion is that there's no such thing. There is, of course, a sort of caricature of a "male" or "female" writing style that can be written by either gender, but the fact that both genders can do the task proves it's phony.

Do you consciously try to deal with the idea of female characters as "the other" or "alien" in your work?

No. To me, it is the male characters who are "other" and "alien." I don't understand them at all. I understand in the Skinnerian sense—that is, after fifty years I understand that if I do X a human male is likely to do Y, but I do not, in even the remotest particular, understand why. Most of the things men do and say mystify me; they might as well be sentient gas clouds. And this idea—males as alien and other—I do deal with consciously and deliberately when I write.

How do you approach developing a character—female or male?

Scientifically, I'm afraid. I don't begin with the character, I begin with the behavior. I want such and such a thing to be done or said or felt in the story; I ask myself, "Now what sort of a person would do/say/feel that? What would such a person be like?" and from the resulting set of characteristics I construct a character.

What is the writing process like from your perspective—do you see yourself as an experimenter, a stylist, a harbinger, an entertainer?

None of the above. If I could be what I wanted to be, in the framework established by your question, I would be a teacher. Teachers explain . . . by example, by demonstration, by overt instruction when that cannot be avoided. I try, in the writing process, to explain. To teach.

Do you ever feel pressured (by fans, by popular culture) to write a certain way?

The terms are wrong, I think. To "feel pressure" sounds as if it were a negative thing. I do feel pressure; I feel the pressure that comes of perceiving a need for an explanation and I feel pressure to fill it. If the need is great, so is the pressure. But I don't see that as negative. I see it as my great good fortune. I never have to worry about what I will write about, or how I will write, because the people I am writing for present me with the set of conditions that constrain the work. If I were going to write a sonnet, I would feel "pressured" to make it fourteen lines, and roughly iambic pentameter, and about a single idea, and so on; but that would not be a burden. It would be a tremendous help, if a sonnet were the goal. I do feel the kind of pressure that I think you are asking about in one regard, the subject of my writing. For example, I attended a panel where women defined by our culture as overweight complained bitterly that no fiction is written with overweight women as positive characters; they considered that to be elitism, and deliberate prejudice from writers. I saw the same gap they saw, and told them so, but I told them that—at least for me—it had nothing to do with deliberate prejudice, it had to do with ignorance. I cannot, out of my own experience, create a believable fat woman as a character. I don't know what it's like. I asked the women for help; I said, "Write to me. Explain to me what it's like." I gave them an example that was suitable for the context; they had complained that no fat woman is ever sent off on a heroic quest, and I told them that I could not write, believably, about the manner in which a fat woman would get either on or off a horse. I just do not have the necessary information. I would like very much to do a novel in which the major character, and a character that would be perceived as positive, would be a fat woman, and I feel pressure about that—but I still don't have the data. I'm a linguist; for me the body language is at least as important as the dialogue, and it has to be right. I read fiction where no human being could possibly perform the actions being described, and I am outraged—I'm not willing to do that. And the body language that goes with being genuinely overweight (and not only the strange displacement of body weight that goes with being very pregnant) is something I don't know anything about. I can't write about it, and I do feel pressure of that kind.

What direction do you see your work taking?

My primary concern is with the concept of resonance, as it applies in physics, in music, in psychology, in linguistics, in theology, in medicine. The next novel I do will be overtly about resonance. Where short stories are concerned, I don't know. I write them in only three situations: when someone I respect has asked me for one, and has given me enough freedom to let me write roughly what I want to write, and has posed an interesting problem to which writing an answer would be a pleasure for me; when I perceive a need to explain that is so urgent that it cannot wait while I write a book; and when I am very very angry, and the story allows me to express that anger and thus not have it contaminating everything else I do. Those situations are not predictable.

Biographical Notes

Suzette Haden Elgin was born and raised in the Ozarks. Suzette majored in linguistics at the University of Chicago;

she married, had numerous children, was widowed, remarried, and had more children. This, she explains, is why it took her from 1954 to 1973 to finish her doctorate in linguistics at the University of California in San Diego.

Ms. Elgin taught at UCSD until she retired to an earth-sheltered house in the Arkansas wilderness. There she runs a variety of micro-industries, including the Ozark Center for Language Studies and The Magic Granny Line, and tends a black walnut grove. Her book *Native Tongue* was a forerunner to the issues addressed in Margaret Atwood's novel *The Handmaid's Tale*.

Books by Suzette Haden Elgin

Native Tongue II: The Judas Rose (DAW Books, 1987)

The Last Word on the Gentle Art of Verbal Self-Defense (Simon & Schuster, 1987)

Yonder Comes the End of Time (DAW Books, 1986)

Star-Anchored (DAW Books, 1984)

Native Tongue (DAW Books, 1984)

The Ozark Trilogy (Berkley Publishing, 1983)

More on the Gentle Art of Verbal Self-Defense (Prentice-Hall, 1983)

The Gentle Art of Verbal Self-Defense (Prentiss-Hall, 1980)

Furthest (Ace Publications, 1971)

The Communipaths (Ace Publications, 1970)

◆

In the Country
of the Mind

Lee Killough

A friend of mine refers to herself as a storyteller rather than a writer. It may be more accurate. A writer could be producing anything, including textbooks and advertising copy, but a storyteller's one product is tales to thrill his listeners, to stir them to laughter or anger or tears, to mystify, delight, and enchant them. And storytelling existed long before writing.

In my own life, certainly, storytelling came well before literacy. Exactly when, I can't recall, but somewhere early. Perhaps the summer my mother and aunt, in an act of madness, or out of mercy for other neighborhood mothers, took on the neighborhood kids. Several times a week they would collect us for a morning or afternoon and take us all on a field trip, to a riding stable or local museum or an animal farm where we

could pet tame skunks and porcupines. Or they orga-
nized group games. One was storytelling. My mother
or aunt started the story, then passed it on to someone
else to continue. At some point, usually when he had
painted himself into a corner, that child handed the
story on to someone else, until everyone in the circle
had a turn. My turn did not stop with the game. I had
also fallen in love with horses that summer and, not
owning or having access to one, I made up another life
in my head that included horses. Sometimes I wanted
to *be* a horse and tried to imagine what it would feel
like to run on four legs and have a tail. At night, after
my mother or father had finished reading the bedtime
story and left my sister and me grumbling at the in-
justice of being expected to go to sleep when it wasn't
even *dark* yet, I shared a little of my private world and
whiled away the twilight by whispering another bedtime story to my sister. Not the most promising of
beginnings for a storyteller, since she almost always
went to sleep in the middle of the tale but, then, those
early stories were about things I liked . . . horses and
cowboys, or episodes of whatever radio show had caught
my fancy at the time: "Sergeant Preston of the Yukon,"
"Wild Bill Hickok," "Dragnet."

Even if my sister did not appreciate that world in
my head, I still loved it. It was much more comfortable
for a shy, awkward child than mixing with other children and risking their rebuffs, so I lived there more and
more. And sources other than radio and television fed
it. For several years, the public library offered a story
hour on Saturday mornings. The head librarian, a tiny
porcelain woman with wire-rimmed glasses and white

hair pulled up into a topknot, sat at the end of a long table in a reading room warm and golden from sunlight filtering through the glass brick walls and read aloud from a book of fairy tales, marvelous stories of magic and dragons, of giants who made themselves immortal by keeping their hearts safe in distant places, of horses who talked and princesses who slipped away into magic lands by night to dance holes in their shoes. The hour always ended too soon. Walking home, I made up similar stories for myself to make the magic last a little longer.

Learning to read gave me access to the worlds in other peoples' heads but, like the story hour, those only fed my own world instead of replacing it. I grumbled at writing exercises, repeating letters over and over for whole pages, but once I mastered it I found a good use for writing. It let me keep my stories in a permanent form; I did not have to worry about forgetting them, and I could go back to them over and over.

By which point storytelling had become an inextricable part of my life. Still, it could have taken many directions—poetry, plays, horse stories. I tried all of them. But then . . .

Then, in junior high school, I finished the very last horse book to be found in either the high school or public libraries. No more horse books! In agony I thumbed through several volumes in the adjoining library section, science fiction, desperately hunting for something else to read. One book looked passably interesting. At least it was not one of the "teen life" books I despised. I took it home to try.

The title is indelibly printed in memory: *The Star-*

men of Llyrdis by Leigh Brackett. So is the name of the second book I tried from that section: *Shambleau and Other Stories*, by C. L. Moore. Fireworks went off in me. It was love at first sight. After devouring a few more books in that section, I was hooked for life, and all the stories in my head became science fiction.

At the time, I never bothered to wonder why; I just wallowed in this breathtaking new literature. But questions from reporters, after I became a professional writer, have made me start to look back to examine the phenomenon. Why *did* science fiction capture me so suddenly and so totally? What about it fulfilled my need for the fantastic? Humankind does crave the fantastic, I believe. Even as our ancestors feared those blank portions of ancient maps labeled "Here Be Dragons" they listened eagerly to every word of the tales of fabulous monsters told by travelers who claimed to know what lay in the blank portions. In the twentieth century the map is filled, yet our appetite for fabulous monsters remains unchanged. We look to uncharted territory elsewhere—inside ourselves, to vampires and werewolves, monsters of our subconscious; to the past, when the world remained uncharted; or forward and outward to the truly uncharted spaces, the stars. Why did I choose the latter? I had loved those fairy stories the librarian read. Why did fantasy, which was scattered through the science-fiction section and offered a universe just as boundless, just as dazzling, now generate only marginal interest?

It is, I have decided, a matter of rationality and possibilities. The wonders of fantasy are clearly imaginary; they can never be "real," and fantasy's wonders

must be accepted for what they are, magic—inexplic-
able except in those terms. Science fiction, on the other
hand, comes with explanations, with gears and wheels
one can peer at to see how the wonders work. And I
was—I *am*—passionately fascinated by how things
work.

I also cherish order, a result, perhaps of growing up
in a world that challenges order on every side and, in
particular, threatens us with the total chaos of nuclear
annihilation. In science fiction, as in mysteries, my
other favorite genre, no matter how chaotic, how baf-
fling the situation at the beginning, it always ends with
explanations found for everything and order established. No wonder science fiction felt like coming home.

It still does, though the types of science fiction I
prefer have changed over the years. Hard science fiction
appealed most in the beginning. I devoured Heinlein,
Asimov, Leinster, and Brackett. *Analog* became my
favorite magazine. It was like being admitted to paradise to make my first sale to that very magazine.

Several years later, when I discovered science-fiction conventions, I heard stories about John Campbell's
alleged male-chauvinist attitudes, implying that, being
female, I was lucky indeed to have sold a story to him.

"But then, you use a name that sounds like a man's,"
someone said.

To which I can only protest that Lee is not a name
I "use"; it happens to *be* my name, albeit my middle
one, and I certainly do not sign my work Lee Killough
to fool John Campbell or any other editor into thinking
I am a man. I happen to like Lee better than my first
name, and think it has a better sound than the hard

alliteration of Karen Killough. I have never made any attempt to hide my sex. My full name is on every manuscript, and most of my books carry a biographical sketch clearly identifying me as female.

On the other hand, I make no point of my sex, either. It is irrelevant to my writing. I am a writer, not a woman writer. Some people claim there is a difference, that women do not write the same way that men do. Bull. The revelation that James Tiptree Jr. was a woman stunned the science-fiction world. "So that's why he wrote such good female characters," people said afterward. But women do not always write good female characters, nor are men incapable of it. Thomas Hardy's best and strongest characters were always women. Women writers don't always use female protagonists, either. Whether mine will be male or female I leave to an intuitive feeling that pokes me somewhere in the process of planning the background and outlining the plot. Dramatic mechanisms and the society of the book's setting may favor a character of one sex or another.

Which is not to deny that I make deliberate choices about characters. Usually, however, it is for effect— playing with role reversal so that a woman rescues a man, or twisting stereotypes to have a woman sticking to procedure and logic while her male companion is brilliantly intuitive—rather than to make a statement. I prefer to confine moralizing to essays and speeches.

Most of the time I let my subconscious deal with developing characterizations—which can be unnerving at times. Those characters develop awesome independence. I recall once trying repeatedly to write a protagonist as male. In vain. Liberty Ibarra just stood there in my head saying firmly, "No. Female." The same may happen with race. After laboring in frustration with the police chief in *Deadly Silents* for half a dozen chapters, I was ready to throw my typewriter across the room. None of his scenes seemed right; he refused to do what I wanted. Then, suddenly, I realized he was black, not caucasian. It was astonishing. Without changing a word of the book except his physical description, now his scenes worked. He came to life and I was comfortable with him. Why, I still cannot figure out; his race made absolutely no difference to the plot. Yet my subconscious insisted Devane Brooks be black and held up the book until I made him so.

My subconscious manages to play a role in the type of stories I write, too. Even as I published my first story in *Analog*, the home of hard science fiction, I realized that the story was only semi-hard science fiction and that my writing was turning in a new direction. I had discovered *The Magazine of Fantasy and Science Fiction*, and J. G. Ballard. Ballard's writing occupied fascinating territory indeed, a half-step out of sync with reality, sprawled across the borderland between fantasy and science fiction. That territory begged for further exploration.

So, for the next several years, I turned out most of my Aventine stories, work heavily influenced by Ballard, in particular his Vermillion Sands series. I like my stories from that period, but I think they are important for more than my personal satisfaction with them. In writing them I realized it is true that people, not gadgets, make stories, and that no technology compares in complexity with the inner workings of people and societies. Aventine also taught me there is fun in more of science fiction than the "rivets and rockets" variety.

I have also discovered pleasures in the very creation process, which have become almost ends in themselves and exist independent of the story itself. This makes my husband sometimes question whether I research in order to write a book or write in order to have an excuse to research and build worlds.

Maybe both. I happily spend weeks compiling the background for a novel—drawing maps, sketching flora and fauna, setting up the ecology, developing the society down to slang words, children's toys, and bathroom fixtures, writing character biographies. I dash in panting eagerness down the often digressing paths opened up by the research. Why did I groan when my teachers used to announce the assignment of a research paper? How *ever* could I have considered research dull? A new project involves a world with mountains to climb, so I not only read everything in the library on mountaineering and catch every assault on Everest broadcast on public television, but enroll in a rock climbing class. Reading about China's Han dynasty in order to model an alien society on it turns me into an avid Sinophile. I start collecting travel and anthropology books about China and Robert van Gulik's series of mystery novels about the real-life eighth-century Chinese magistrate Judge Dee. Brushing up on history to see how people lived in fifteenth-century Russia plunges me not only into Russian history, but into Tolstoy's writing and generates extensive reading on contemporary Russia.

My husband can tease me all he likes; I savor the delights of digression without guilt. None of it is wasted since it all serves to increase my knowledge and broaden my horizons, a basic necessity for a writer. How can I create new worlds without building material? How can I write except out of myself? Consider creativity as recombinant DNA. Everything I read, see, and hear breaks up into component pieces in the stewpot in my subconscious. It's a stew best made thick; one never knows what components of which unrelated pieces of knowledge will bump into each other and rise to the surface as a viable idea.

"What if . . ." it will whisper in my ear. I snatch at the idea glittering there on the edge of consciousness and am off. What if there were intelligent beings who could fly? What if a race of telepaths existed? What would they be like? What would their societies be like? What if someone with a multiple personality disorder was accepted in society? If vampires existed, what might they *really* be like? Would being a cop, working a night shift in a tough section of town, be the perfect means to blend a werewolf into human society?

The storyteller is an experimenter, a tinkerer, stretching physical laws, redesigning societies to let something exist for the purpose of the plot. One can see what it is like to be God. The Fundamentalists have it wrong. A god cannot treat characters like puppets, pulling the strings for every move. If I *really* want to see what would happen in this situation or that society, my characters have to be allowed free will, total freedom, even to dig themselves into pits and die. At most, I can only nudge here and there.

At best, that is all I have to do. Given that my world is viable and the population realistic, the characters caper beyond my control anyway, like Devane Brooks and Liberty Ibarra.

A good many of my story ideas are not what-if whispers but images. Out of nowhere comes a picture—a scene, a portrait. There are no words, no explanations. I am left to puzzle out the meaning for myself. Where is this place? Who are these people? What are they doing?

Images dominate my writing process. Perhaps because I came to storytelling before learning to write, I always see the stories as they happen. They play out in my head, a world in miniature, complete with sounds and smells, and I have to make a conscious effort to put them into words. Images play a prominent role in the planning of a story, too. I think best with a pen in my hand, doodling, sketching. None of my background books are complete without copious diagrams of flora, fauna, aliens, and floor plans.

In fact, the first skill I had to develop as a writer was translating images from nonverbal experiences in my head to words on paper. It was not always easy. I may know perfectly well how a sword sounds withdrawing from its scabbard, but how do I accurately describe that particular blend of hiss and ring? How do I name the sound a horse makes by fluttering its nostrils when confronted by something it considers highly suspicious? Not as a snort. Snorts are short. Not as a neigh or scream or nicker. One would think that after the thousands of years we have associated with the horse, we would have a word for every part of it, for every movement and sound. I made up a word: whuffle. I thought I made it up. Recently an English girl informed me that she has always called the sound a whiffle.

Describing odors is worse, of course. We have *no* definitive vocabulary for scents. Sweet, acrid, foul, sharp, and so on are hardly exact. They cannot convey to a listener or reader the nuances of the scent I imagine so clearly. The best we can do is compare the smell to a familiar one. The scent is like vanilla, we say, or it is fruity with a hint of spice. At this point, we begin to sound like wine tasters.

Some images do not immediately suggest a plot line. They float around in the back of my head, mysterious and tantalizing. An image appears of a white beach with red footprints crossing it. I know how the footprints were made: as the white sand is very fine and the red sand coarse and heavy, stepping on the sand drives one's foot through to the layer beneath, so the footprint shows red until the white gradually sifts back into the depression. I do not know who left the tracks, however, nor why such a beach exists. Nor do I learn, no matter how long I puzzle over the image. Ideas have their time. Some have to ripen. The beach haunts me for years before the view suddenly expands and I see that it's an alien garden rather than a beach, and not really a garden but a stage set. Eventually, that image of the red footprints opens and closes "Bete et Noir," another story in the Aventine series.

There is a pattern in the ideas I write about. Just as the child I was made up radio and television episodes that I enjoyed, the writer I have become continues to choose subjects that interest me over ones that are commercially popular. If two subjects interest me equally, I like to combine them. Perhaps that is why the borderlands continually fascinate me. I do love that territory between science fiction and fantasy, between science fiction and mystery. The Aventine stories come from there, and all my books mix science fiction with mystery, including one novelette in which the detective is a ghost. There is a vampire novel, too, but one that is more of a police procedural than a horror story, and Garreth Doyle Mikaelian—Irish-American, blond, gray-eyed, a bit overweight (to start with)—is very unlike the image of most vampires. Animal and plant breeding programs benefit from the hybrid vigor of crossbreeding; why not literature?

More and more, though, choosing a subject becomes more difficult as research for new stories introduces me to ideas I would like to write about. The human consequences of new technology intrigue me. Embryo transplants are routine, successful procedures in cattle, and becoming increasingly more so in horses. How might it affect society if humans adopt the technique on a widespread basis, not just for women who cannot carry a pregnancy to term, but for career or personal convenience? I enjoy experimenting with viewpoints and character stereotypes. What if we tell a dragon versus knight story from the dragon's side? Or write a fantasy using mythology other than that we are familiar with in western culture? African, for instance. Ancient West African empires had complex structure, sophisticated codes of chivalry, and epics as grand as Homer's. Africa has a whole new set of monsters, too. Most people are visually oriented. What might it be like to do a story from a blind protagonist's point of view, giving the reader no visual imagery at all, only sound and scent and tactile sensations? What about having a beautiful, genuinely charming villain and an ugly hero? Reptiles are looked on with distaste by most people. They turn up in science fiction as villains or, at most, as cuted-up sidekicks. Is it possible to make a genuinely reptilian being sympathetic, even admirable?

Experimentation is always chancy, of course. The result may be well written and yet not commercial. I had a short-story idea once, set in the world of my book *Voice Out of Ramah*. Ninety percent of the boys die when they reach puberty, owing to an ancient bacterial weapon that turns male hormones to poison. That being the case, a woman might ensure her son's life by castrating him. But this is a society dominated by religion and a belief in bowing to God's will. How would the rest of society look on this woman, and on her son? What would he feel about himself?

I never wrote the story because I was afraid no editor would buy a story about the problems of a castrated boy. Perhaps I was wrong to be timid. I had difficulty marketing the nonhorror vampire novel. Editors liked it but could not decide how to categorize it. Cross-genre books run that risk. The marketplace likes categorization. I can see the point; it makes advertising and bookstore shelving easier. Yet the vampire novel did sell. Might my castrated boy have also found a buyer eventually? And, even if not, did I deprive myself of valuable experience by not trying the story anyway? How else can a writer grow except by experimenting, by trying something new, stretching? The one romance novel I've written never sold, but I don't consider it a waste of time. The experience was interesting. It taught me a whole new writing style, and I take some pride in the fact that I learned it well enough for the editors to comment favorably on the writing style and invite further submissions even as they rejected that particular book.

Perhaps I will write that story about the castrated boy one day. After all, what is a storyteller or science-fiction writer who takes no chances? I don't love the genre for playing safe. That is not what science fiction is about. Exploration *is*, playing with imagination, examining possibilities, making the impossible plausible. The science-fiction universe spreads out before me, its wild, shadowy borderlands and wilderness footpaths calling. If anyone comes looking for me, tell them I went "out there."

Biographical Notes

Lee Killough has spent most of her life in small Kansas towns, she reports, but only in body. Her parents gave her an ideal start by instilling in her the love of reading. Both of them worked with language; her father teaching English and Spanish, her mother working as a journalist. They loved books and often read aloud to their children. Perhaps most helpful of all, the household remained televisionless until Ms. Killough was in junior high school.

Her writing hobby turned into a profession after she married Howard Patrick Killough in 1966 and he urged her to submit her work for publication. She calls him "My best and most severe critic." She also claims her nonwriting job keeps her in the proper mindset for creating science fiction.

As chief technologist in radiology at the Kansas State University Veterinary Medical Center in Manhattan, Kansas, she deals with nonhuman species every day. Ms. Killough has seven books in print. One of her short stories, "Symphony for a Lost Traveler," was nominated for the Hugo award in 1985.

Books by Lee Killough

Bloodlinks (Tor, 1988)

The Leopard's Daughter (Warner, 1987)

Blood Hunt (Tor, 1987)

Spider Play (Warner, 1986)

Liberty's World (DAW, 1985)

Aventine (Del Rey, 1982)

Deadly Silents (Del Rey, 1981)

The Monitor, the Miners, and the Shree (Del Rey, 1980)

The Doppelganger Gambit (Del Rey, 1979)

A Voice Out of Ramah (Del Rey, 1979)

ONE WOMAN'S EXPERIENCE IN SCIENCE FICTION

Marion Zimmer Bradley

I have often heard the conventional wisdom about women in science fiction; namely, that there aren't any, or weren't before 1961. There's just one thing wrong with the conventional wisdom; it isn't true.

For some reason women just don't want to believe it; the late Alice Sheldon wrote under a male pen name (James Tiptree Jr.) for much of her writing life; Rachel Cosgrove Payes wrote under the pen name E. R. Arch, "because everybody knows a woman can't get published under a female name." Women made much of the fact that Alice Mary Norton became Andre Norton, Catherine L. Moore used the initials C. L. and Leigh Brackett and I both had gender-irrelevant names. (I didn't even know this; in our family Marion has always been a woman's name, just as no one would ever have sug-

gested to my father that Leslie *was* a woman's name.)
Dorothy Bryant once excused her vanity publishing to
me "because everyone knows a woman can't get published in science fiction and fantasy." When I said I'd
never had any trouble, she told me I had "sold out to
the male establishment." I don't quite know what she
meant; maybe that I wrote what people wanted to read
instead of cramming tracts on feminism down their
throats. If that's selling out, I plead guilty.

The truth about the dearth of women in science
fiction is that the *audience* identified with male values.
In the thirties, when science fiction had its beginnings
(except for such prehistoric writers as H. G. Wells and
Jules Verne), the readership of science fiction was as
carefully targeted as viewers of the Western—men
and boys, and occasionally women and girls who did
not care to read what was supposedly appropriate to
their sex (which in those days consisted mostly of
romances).

One could say that the women writers who were
always there were in some way driven. After all, women
had always been active in fantasy fiction. Mary Woll-
stonecraft Shelley wrote one of the first novels on a
fantasy subject: *Frankenstein, or the New Prometheus.*
In those days, before the movies got hold of the monster, the emphasis was more on the character of the
monster and his feelings of alienation—always a great
fantasy theme. In the twenties, there was a famous
fantasy: *Angel Island,* by Inez Haynes Irwin, which
proved, without alienating the male audience for whom
it was written, to be a most powerful metaphor of feminism. There were many others: the original horror

story, *The Angel Island* is the story of winged women, who upon reaching adulthood have their wings cut off. *Castle of Udolpho*, was written by a Mrs. Ann Radcliffe. Why did these women step outside the field of comfortable domestic fiction—which included *Jane Eyre* and the many works where the heroine exists only to suffer and/or find a husband—that was the supposed province of their sex? I can speak only of the women I have known, and I can only imagine that they were in some way driven. In my own experience, I was so bored by "girls' books" that I read "boys' adventure stories." When the time came for me to start writing, I wrote the kind of thing I liked to read: adventure stories. I never met an editor who cared whether I was a man, a woman, a little girl, or a chimpanzee— as long as I could write the kind of story they wanted to read.

Let us return to the issue of male pen names. C. L. Moore told me once that she had adopted initials because had she published her first story, the classic *Shambleau*, under her own name, she might have lost her job as a bank teller. In 1933, the depths of the Depression, Ms. Moore was the only working member of her family and the sole support of her aging parents; she did not wish to risk her livelihood on the uncertain business of fiction writing. By the time C. L. Moore was well known enough to write full-time, everybody recognized the pen name and knew that it belonged to a woman. The same thing happened to the well-known writer of Westerns, Bertha M. Bower. In her case editors and publishers believed that the ordinary male audience would question a woman's knowledge of cowpunchers. So Bertha became B. M., but every editor in the business knew her true sex as did every reader who was interested—not many of them were.

Then we come to the field of Weird Tales—the genre and the magazine, which was always the most prestigious of the pulps. In addition to printing such "greats" as H. P. Lovecraft, Fritz Leiber, and Robert Bloch, it was edited, for many years after the death of Farnsworth Wright, by the knowledgeable Dorothy McIlwraith. *Famous Fantastic Mysteries* was edited by Mary Gnaedinger. One of the finest editors in the business, Mary also presented Inez Irwin's *Angel Island* without protest from the mostly male audience of the forties. And then there was Leigh Brackett.

It is rather difficult to write of Leigh Brackett; in addition to being my role model, she was a close and much-loved friend. Leigh began writing in the forties—actually just before the start of the forties; she made her *Planet Stories* debut in 1939. She was a great admirer of Raymond Chandler and wrote more than one hard-boiled detective story. Pamela Sargent presented the feminist view of Leigh Brackett in the preface to *Women of Wonder*: "She writes like a male, and a male steeped in machismo at that." As a student of every word Leigh has written, I disagree. With all due respect to Pamela Sargent, she knows nothing of the realities of writing in that day. Leigh wrote of what she saw; she filled the perceived needs of the marketplace instead of slaving somewhere as a schoolteacher or a waitress and writing the Great Feminist Novel at night. This is selling out to the male establishment; readers will look in vain for any trace of "machismo" in her books, and Leigh never made any secret of her sex. Everyone in science fiction knew her gender by 1946, when I came into the field.

So what of this accusation that Leigh writes "like a man steeped in machismo"? I personally never saw any hint of it. True, her stories told of the dealings of men; so did mine, and no one ever said that about *me*. *All* science-fiction stories in the forties and fifties were about men; Leigh could not have sold them otherwise. Had she chosen to write solely about women, she could only have published them at a vanity press. I think that would have damaged her credibility as a writer. Leigh Brackett wrote of female characters who appeared— even in her early hard-boiled stories—as independent self-determined women. Women were not exploited by men in Leigh's stories. Leigh told me once "if I had a woman in a story at all, she was *doing* something, not worrying about the price of eggs or who's in love with whom."

Leigh was often trashed by feminists, and like me, she didn't give a damn. Leigh was once invited to a feminist film festival. Rather than honoring her for making it in the most fiercely competitive of fields, where men are defeated daily, the women chose to attack Leigh for "cooperating with the male establishment" and not making lots of small, noncommercial feminist films, all of which were pretty dreadful. I think these self-righteous feminists, if they were as true to themselves as Leigh was to herself, would have admitted the possibility that most feminist films do not make it into the mainstream because they are just not very good.

I admit that I am prejudiced against feminism—or all card-carrying isms. I feel very strongly that trying to mix art with politics makes for bad art and bad politics. Why is it that artists who are the pampered darlings of the communist system are always defecting to the West in order to write (or dance, or sing, or compose) "free" art?

Then there is Andre Norton. In Andre's case it is even simpler; she was not deliberately trying to conceal her sex. Another Alice Mary Norton was already a famous writer of children's books in England. Andre, a librarian, knew the Borrowers books well, and wished to avoid confusion. As for me, as I've said, I did not know that Marion was an ambiguous name. For that matter, you can still find boys named Evelyn (my mother's name) or Beverly in England.

Lee Hoffman passed herself off as a boy all through her life in fandom, in order to reveal her gender with a "bang" at the first New Orleans convention. Her real name was *Shirley*. I guessed her true sex, and at her request kept it a secret. I guessed she was a woman when in a letter she wrote me, she said she had to stop and go run some clothes through the mangle. While a boy might help his mother with the laundry, I knew that a boy would not have given it as a reason for not writing sooner. Lee later became modestly well-known as a writer of "Ranch Romances"—a field where even rodeo queens do not have enough credibility to write Western novels. Perhaps this is because of the related field of "Ranch Romances"—love stories with a faintly Western background.

Like most readers of science fiction, I do not generally admire romances. Rebecca Brandywyne, who recently wrote a romance with fantasy elements, *Passion Moon Rising*, raises several good questions: Why should we put down romances as an inferior genre, or "quasi-pornography," when we are all writers of genre fiction? Why should a writer of one type of genre fiction put down another? I feel, as I think most writers feel, that a writer of romances is perpetuating a negative stereotype. Romances perpetuate the image of women who are concerned *before anything else* with getting the attentions of a "valuable" man. This stereotype, of course, is not unknown in science fiction. Larry Niven and Jerry Pournelle, authors of the otherwise excellent *Lucifer's Hammer*, included in that novel a passage that made me see red. They explain that the comet that nearly destroyed civilization had brought an end to women's liberation, that women would get status as they always had—from the powerful men to whom they were attached. To find this idea in a book written by a *woman* is—to me, at least—disgusting and pornographic. According to my standards, it's okay for a woman in a story to have whatever love life suits her, but the real work of the world must come first. That is the brand of feminism I cling to.

What then is a female writer to hope for if romances bore her to tears and writing adventure stories brings accusations of "writing like a man, and a man steeped in *machismo* at that"?

Let us first address that bugaboo of adventure-story writers. The ordinary well-plotted story is subject to the idea that plot is a masculist device invented to exploit women. On the surface there is a sort of specious logic to this; after all, most plots make their way through a climax to some sort of conclusion. Well, assuming, for argument's sake, that only men have climaxes (an argument at which a lot of women, including sexologists, would giggle if not guffaw), must we therefore write stories (which some feminists do) in which "Womyn" go around having a lot of good feelings about one another, without conflict and without climax? I think not; stories written by men as well as women can be plotted to avoid offense to women. A story need not turn on romance or marriage as a plot point. There are only three basic conflicts on which a story may turn:

1. Man against nature
2. Man against man
3. Man against himself

Only in the second of these do we find the romance theme overwhelming; but there are, for story purposes, many things that can take place between man and man—or for that matter man against woman—other than romance or marriage. One can focus on equality, power, revenge.

Some attempts to write typical women's fiction within the context of science fiction have worked and some haven't. One successful attempt was Judith Merril's best-seller of the early forties, *Shadow on the Hearth*. In this classic, Merril tells the story of a housewife fighting a traditionally female battle against nuclear war. I have no idea why this story was not published in the *Ladies' Home Journal*, for it deals mostly with the traditional concerns of a woman in such a conflict; her children have radiation sickness, her toaster won't work because the electricity is off, her son is drafted into the army, a lecherous neighbor is making passes at her—and all she wants is for her husband to come home. Before I say anything critical I should say that I greatly admire Judith Merril, and while her book presents what seems to me an awfully myopic view of nuclear war, she does address the concerns of a certain kind of woman—the suburban housewife. The works of Jane Gaskell include a heroine—I use the word advisedly—who is vulnerable to rape, childbirth, and adventures at the hands of lecherous heroes. I don't like these stories much, but they are very popular. Rebecca Brandywyne's attempt to combine the fantasy and romance genres may be filling a need for some readers; the haggis shortage is not yet imminent. (This relates to the old Scottish saying: "It's a good thing we haven't all the same tastes, think of the haggis shortage there'd be.")*

When I came into the field, nobody spoke of prejudice existing against women, except that it was expected that women would have to be about twice as good as men. I'm accustomed to that; every woman who wanted to go to medical school—at least up until the forties—simply accepted (and didn't waste time whining about it) that she'd have to be twice as good as a man. Some women may have resented this in secret, but most of us revelled in the thought that we'd made it against terrific odds, and took it as proof that

---

*Editor's note: Haggis is a Scottish pudding.

we were at least twice as good as the men. ("Fortunately," some feminist said, "that's not difficult.")

Then something changed. The success of *Star Trek* showed that at least half the audience out there—maybe more—was female. D. C. Fontana—Dorothy, who chose her pen name more for luck than gender—said once, flippantly, that half of her job as producer was in giving the lovely Nichelle Nichols (as Lieutenant Uhura) "something more to do than opening hailing frequencies." Little girls were just as responsive to *Star Trek* as little boys. Most of the active *Star Trek* enthusiasts were women—Joan Winston, Bjo Trimble, and Jacqueline Lichtenberg, who gained a reputation writing *Star Trek* fiction, and then moved on to her own work. Jacqueline is neither the first nor the only; my own anthologies made special use of the women who had made their reputations writing *Star Trek* or sometimes Darkover fiction.

Late in the fifties, Cele Goldsmith had been the editor of *Amazing Stories*, and the excellent editor Judy-Lynn Benjamin—better known as Judy-Lynn Del Rey—became the expert and knowledgeable assistant to John W. Campbell at *Analog*. Then, about the same time as *Star Trek*, came the explosion of women in science fiction. The women had been there all along, of course; but before this, the most *active* fans were active because they had a husband or a brother in the movement. Suddenly women were everywhere.

These were the years in which my own fiction took a quantum leap from ordinary adventure fiction—*Star of Danger* and similar stories—to in-depth explorations of women's issues. I had always written of strong and independent women, who were not there to "worry about the price of eggs or who's in love with whom." In *Winds of Darkover*, Melora—who started out as the traditional female heroine, with her castle under seige by bandits—courageously rescues herself and her family. From there I went on (under the courageous editorship of Don Wollheim, my mentor in all things) to explore issues in depth. *Heritage of Hastur*, one of my best-known books, dealt with the self-acceptance of a homosexual; *Shattered Chain*, another landmark book, dealt with a woman's independence. Oddly enough, *Shattered Chain*, which Don Wollheim called "hard core feminism," was attacked by feminists, as was my later book, *The Ruins of Isis*, on the grounds that "Bradley is evidently[!] not equal to the challenge of an all female society." I must say sales figures are an ample vindication; *Shattered Chain* has been read, and thought about, by men and women who would have pitched the more classically (and politically correct) feminist tract *The Female Man* across the room. One cannot really prove anything by sales figures, however. I do not write for best-sellerdom (after all, the best-seller list usually includes the latest pop trash, such as diet books or the romantic confessions of some superstar). However, my sales figures at least show that I have reached a large segment of the existing readership.

In writing this essay I have been asked to give the reasons that I write, and the reasons I have chosen to be known as a science-fiction and fantasy writer. In response I would say that in fantasy there are no brakes on the imagination. In a recent supreme-court case in Tennessee, some parents sought to ban such fantasy as *The Wizard of Oz* on the grounds that "these children's imaginations have got to be restrained." Fantasy spoke well of witches; these people considered them a danger to religion. I take my stand firmly against such restrictions. When people say the pilgrim fathers came here for religious freedom, they really refer to a freedom from an established religion. We cannot run our country for the Fundamentalists. Their religion works only so long as they do not try to force it on people who have a view of the world that is too large to be contained in any book—even the Bible.

Not that I am an irreligious person. On the contrary, I feel very strongly that there is a certain amount of blasphemy in limiting human imagination. If (as materialists say) there is no difference between man and animal, imagination is just another function of the "black box" that is the brain. If God made us special, different from the animals, it is the imagination that sets us apart. When we attempt to deny it, we are denying God's place in the world of the mind. Who would say that it's better to write about adultery in the suburbs, football, or corruption in high places than to create fantasy? There are a lot of books on these other subjects; I don't say there is no place for them, but I think they are pretty dull. I can see them when I look all about me. In science fiction we are forced to think about the future—to believe there will *be* a future. Thus science fiction is the only field that addresses itself (despite occasional messengers of gloom and doom via the cautionary tale) to the survival of the human race. Fantasy forces us to confront our own archetypes—what lives eternally in the human mind.

◆   *Marion Zimmer Bradley*

Biographical Notes

Marion Zimmer Bradley was born and raised in Albany, New York. She attended New York State College for Teachers, Hardin-Simmons College, where she received her B.A., and has done graduate work at the University of California at Berkeley.

Mrs. Zimmer Bradley began writing and publishing stories in 1953; her early influences were Theodore Sturgeon and Catherine L. Moore. She has been nominated several times for Hugo awards and was the recipient of the 1984 *Locus* award for her novel, *The Mists of Avalon*. This best-seller, along with other highly acclaimed works, such as the Darkover series, attest to her increasing popularity and marketability. Marion Zimmer Bradley currently resides in Berkeley, California.

Selected Books by Marion Zimmer Bradley

The Firebrand (Simon & Schuster, 1987)

The Other Side of the Mirror and Other Darkover Stories (DAW Books, 1987)

The Winds of Darkover (Ace, 1985)

The Inheritor (Tom Doherty Associates, 1984)

The Colors of Space (Pocket Books, 1983)

The Web of Darkness (Baen, 1983)

The Mists of Avalon (Knopf, 1982)

House Between The Worlds (Doubleday, 1980)

Stormqueen (Ace, 1980)

The Catch Trap (Ballantine Books, 1979)

The Survivors (DAW Books, 1979)

The Ruins of Isis (Pocket Books, 1978)

The Forbidden Tower (DAW Books, 1977)

The Shattered Chain (DAW Books, 1976)

The Heritage of Hastur (DAW Books, 1975)

The Spell Sword (DAW Books, 1974)

The Brass Dragon (Ace Books, 1969)

The Bloody Sun (Ace Books, 1964)

The Sword of Aldones (Gregg Press, 1962)

The Planet Savers (Ace, 1962)

The Door Through Space (Ace Books, 1961)

◆

ON WRITING SCIENCE FICTION

Eleanor Arnason

If I close my eyes, I can see the house where I spent most of my childhood. It was 1940s modern: redwood walls and huge picture windows. The floors were covered with black-and-white marble patterned linoleum. The kitchen was full of stainless steel.

Most of the furniture was modern, designed by Mies van der Rohe, Alvar Aalto, Isamu Noguchi, and Charles Eames. It came from the museum where my father worked. The museum owned the house, which had been built as a design project shortly after the end of World War II. My parents rented the house, furnished.

My mother had some nineteenth-century American furniture that had come from her family, plus a lot of knickknacks from China. Her parents had been missionaries. She had spent her early childhood in Szechwan and had graduated from the American High School in Shanghai.

(She told me about finding the footprints of leopards in the snow near their summer place in the mountains of Szechwan. She told me about her high school friend in Shanghai, who had been seduced by an American sailor, gotten pregnant, and committed suicide.)

The Victorian and Chinese stuff was mixed in with the chairs and tables by Aalto and Eames. There was plenty of art in the house, most of it done by people my father knew, and there were a lot of books.

My parents were both passionate readers. My mother loved the novels of Dickens and Jane Austen. She owned two complete editions of Dickens and stray third copies of most of the novels. My father liked Henry Fielding, T.S. Eliot and Robert W. Service. When I was very young, he used to drive my brother and me to school. He recited poetry on the way. To this day, I know large chunks of "The Love Song of J. Alfred Prufrock," "The Cremation of Sam McGee," and "The Shooting of Dan McGrew."

I don't know when I began writing. I know that I was telling stories before I was able to read and playing with my brother elaborate games that involved an entire society of plastic barnyard animals. The animals were on Mars, safely away from human beings. I remember that clearly.

A lot of kids tell stories. Maybe all kids do. Any kid who loves books is going to try to write. I think I kept writing because of my mother. There was nothing in her life more important than books. But she did not write. She believed she lacked something: creativity, the divine spark. She thought I had it. She praised me for writing, encouraged me, and gave me a lot of good criticism—not harsh, but intelligent and fair.

It's as simple as that. I wrote because I came from a family of book lovers. I wrote because my mother was a frustrated author. I wrote because it got me attention. I wrote because I wanted to tell stories.

Why science fiction?

I grew up on fairy tales, as do most kids, I guess. I loved science fiction from the moment I discovered it on television; "Captain Video" was definitely my favorite show.

My taste in poetry has always been respectable. The poets I read in high school were the ones who are taught in English classes in college. But I liked popular fiction, too: Sherlock Holmes, Arsene Lupin, Tarzan and John Carter, the detective stories of Dashiell Hammett, the westerns of Max Brand, the historical romances of Georgette Heyer.

Most especially, I liked popular fiction that was set outside the ordinary world. Maybe I was escaping, though I don't remember the science fiction that I read in the 1950s as being particularly comforting. I remember lots of stories set in police states and in radioactive wastelands.

Maybe I turned to science fiction not to escape the world I found myself in, but to understand it. My life as a child was, in many ways, fluid, discontinuous, made up of odd bits and pieces: my mother's stories about China, my father's stories about Iceland, my own experiences traveling. By the time I was seven, I had lived in New York, Chicago, Washington, D.C., London, Paris, St. Paul, and Minneapolis.

I lived through a good part of World War II, through the cold war and the McCarthy-era and the witch hunts. All of this was fairly strange.

I lived daily with the wonders of technology. Our house was an idea house. That was its name: Idea House Number Two. It had been built as wave-of-the-future domestic architecture, the kind of house that used to appear in *Life Magazine* right after the war: "Now that we have beaten the Nazis, this is what we have to look forward to." We had electric heat, central air conditioning, a garbage disposal, all the most up-to-date appliances. In 1949, we got a television.

I also lived daily with the dangers of technology. I can't remember a time when I wasn't afraid of nuclear war.

Maybe that was what I used science fiction for—to deal with cultures that did not fit together, with a rapidly changing society, with the obvious wonders and dangers of technology.

Maybe I was escaping as well. Minnesota in the 1950s was boring. I mean, think of what the Fifties were like everywhere, and then think about what the Midwest is like. Take *Happy Days* and cross it with a Garrison Keillor monologue about Lake Wobegon and ask yourself, would you want to spend five minutes in such a place?

Minnesota was also scary. Terrible menaces loomed over me—Joe McCarthy and Mr. Bomb. I was powerless.

It was a relief to turn to a kind of fiction that didn't bore me and didn't make me feel like a victim. Science-fiction heroes overcame witch hunters and crypto-fascists. They survived the bomb. They moved through the glowing ruins of Earth with competence.

The stories I told before I could read were all fantastic. My daydreams in high school were space opera. My first novel—written when I was sixteen—concerned a lost civilization in Africa. The protagonist in my novel was male. So were all the important characters in my stories and daydreams. Women could not do—or be—anything interesting.

(I can remember being upset when I was about fifteen, because I wanted to be a poet—a really good one—and everyone knew that women were never good poets. At the time, my favorite poet was Emily Dickinson.)

All through the 1950s and most of the 1960s, I wrote about men. They were outlaws and exiles, people who didn't fit in. My anger came out in their stories, as did my sense of alienation. Like them, I was living on someone else's planet. I don't think it ever occurred to me that these people, who were full of *my* emotions, ought to be women. After all, I was a woman, though I didn't like to think about it.

Part of the problem was that I was writing science fiction. The few women writers in the field hid behind initials or androgynous names. The few women characters were icky. Remember Helen O'Loy?

Women characters were loving robots and conscientious housewives, who worried about yellow waxy buildup as they sped toward the stars. Sultry alien women. There was no one here I could identify with.

I moved to Detroit in 1968, the year after the Detroit uprising. I moved—at least in part—in order to get away from the middle-class white society that had surrounded me all my life. What better place than Motown, which was half black and overwhelmingly blue collar? In this same period, I discovered the women's movement. It was a rough time. I couldn't even talk to the people I met at work. I was too white, too middle class, too intellectual. I had to learn a new way of talking and thinking. Outside work, I spent hours in rap groups and with my friends, discussing what it meant to be a woman. I remember being continually angry for months.

Sometime in this period, I wrote an epic poem. It was an allegory, set in the world of Spenser's *Faerie Queene*, full of characters with names like Hope, Greed, Charity, Despondency, and Idle Delight. The title of the poem was "The Amazon." The main character was a "lady knight" descended from the Amazons of Greek mythology.

I decided that the poem would have an equal number of male and female characters, and that the good guys and bad guys would be equally split between female and male.

I made a list with four headings: good characters, male; bad characters, male; good characters, female; bad characters, female.

Every time I added a new character, I decided whether the character was good or evil, then I looked at my list.

If the character was good, and the last good character was female, then this one was male.

I think I made a few exceptions to this rule. Hope and Charity are traditionally female. I stuck with tradition. Greed—an allegorical representation of industrial capitalism—seemed male to me.

Even with the exceptions, the technique served its purpose. It broke me of the habit of making all the important characters male. I've been thinking of using it again in order to get more people of color into my stories, also more gay men and lesbians. Maybe I should be thinking about including people with major handicaps.

The characters in science fiction tend to be like the people on television. They are mostly young and mostly white. Their culture is western. Their health is pretty good.

We'll write about other kinds of people to make a point. A story idea may require that people be old or sick or green or poor or not very bright. But we don't have a good sense of the ordinary everyday diversity of human beings. Maybe we should work on that.

After I started writing about women, my fiction got a lot better, and I became a lot more prolific. I started to get published in the early 1970s.

I belong to the Biodegradable Generation: the writers who appeared between 1969 and 1974.

I pick these dates arbitrarily or, more accurately, for personal reasons. *The Left Hand of Darkness* came out in 1969. *The Dispossessed* came out in 1974. A lot of my writing in this period was done in the shadow of Ursula K. Le Guin. I was influenced as well by the stories in *Orbit* and *New Worlds*.

I had the usual interests for a member of the generation of the early 1970s: anthropology, psychology, sociology, political theory, the woman question, the environment. I had, as well, an interest in the relationship of art to reality.

Remember that I grew up around books and art.

Remember that I was a woman, who needed to know what being a woman meant.

Remember that I had watched the Twin Cities Metropolitan Area spread out and out, over good farmland. Marshes were filled in. Lawn grass replaced meadows and woods.

These experiences had an effect on my writing.

I don't think my reasons for loving science fiction and writing it have changed much over the years. I still write in order to understand my life, which continues to be fluid and discontinuous, full of odd bits and pieces.

I am still fascinated by the wonders of technology. I am still terrified of the dangers.

I still write to escape boredom and despair.

But I want my escape to be temporary. I want my fiction to lead me and my readers back to the reality of everyday life.

I realize that I have said nothing about fantasy.

My first novel, *The Sword Smith*, was marketed as fantasy. There is no magic in it. I tend to think of it as science fiction. My third novel, *Daughter of the Bear*

King, is clearly a fantasy, though the publisher has labeled it science fiction. Both books have dragons and flush toilets.

It is not always easy to distinguish the two categories of fiction.

Brian Aldiss argues that science fiction came into existence as a separate kind of literature in the nineteenth century. I think he's right, and I think the same is true of fantasy.

Nonrealistic literature has a long history. There are myths, legends, fairy tales, animal stories, fabulous journeys, romances, and so on.

I don't think modern fantasy has much to do with any of this. It often uses the old props, but it uses them in a new way. Like science fiction, modern fantasy is a product of the Industrial Revolution. It has a lot more to do with Victorian gothic than it does with the real Middle Ages.

(When I come to think of it, *The Lord of the Rings* is very much like a Victorian cathedral, rising in the middle of an industrial city, the smoke from the factories twisting around the gargoyles.)

Science fiction deals with the effect of science and technology on people. Fantasy deals with the things that have been devalued in industrial society: emotion, intuition, personal loyalty, the sense that human society is organic and cooperative, the sense that human beings are part of the natural world. Both are ways to analyze the changes caused by industrialization, to understand what has been lost and what has been gained. Both are also escape reading for the people trapped in factories, offices, and laboratories.

They developed in tandem, at least in America. They are marketed together, in the same racks in the bookstores. Usually the racks are labeled "science fiction."

A lot of writers move back and forth between the two categories. A lot of books sit right on the dividing line. Are the John Carter books fantasy or science fiction? Remember how John got to Mars? What about the stories of Leigh Brackett? Or Marion Zimmer Bradley?

Maybe I ought to call this essay *On Writing Science Fiction and Fantasy*.

But I haven't.

Biographical Notes

Eleanor Arnason was born in New York City and was raised in Minneapolis. She attended Swarthmore College, where she received an undergraduate degree in art history. Ms. Arnason attended the University of Minnesota and continued graduate courses in her major. She is the secretary-treasurer of the local chapter of the National Writer's Union. Her current writing project is a pair of closely related science fiction books: *In the Light of Sigma Draconis* and *Changing Women*, both due out in 1989.

Eleanor has been the Guest of Honor at several science-fiction conventions. She currently resides in Minneapolis and writes full-time.

Books by Eleanor Arnason

Daughter of the Bear King (Avon Books, 1987)
To The Resurrection Station (Avon Books, 1986)
The Sword Smith (Condor Publishing, 1978)

◆

THE RESTLESS URGE TO WRITE

Joan D. Vinge

There used to be an ad for the Famous Writers School that ran on matchbook covers. It read, *Do You Have the Restless Urge to Write?* Whenever I think about my career as a writer, it always comes back into my mind, because it seems to sum up creativity better than anything I've seen. I never expected to become a science-fiction writer; probably no one was more surprised about it than I was. And yet I've had a restless urge to create *something*—not always in the form of writing—and share it, ever since childhood.

My mother discovered that when I was barely three I lay in bed at night making up stories to put myself to sleep. (A habit I continued into adulthood.) I remember that most of the stories were about cowboys; sometimes I tried to make their action fit the background music of whatever show my parents were watching on the television downstairs. (I am a "night person," and always had trouble getting to sleep at night, even as a child. My daily period of peak creativity generally runs between three in the afternoon and three in the morning, which can be inconvenient in a nine-to-five world.)

When I was about eight years old I fell in love with horses, and also began to draw, suddenly and rather compulsively. From then on I drew and painted pictures of horses and people and other things, but mostly horses. In junior high school, my horse-crazy friends and I used to spend our spare time in the library, reading about horses and writing our own stories about them, which we rarely finished. I would illustrate everyone's stories with my pictures. The drawing was more important to me then than the writing, and I began to imagine rather vaguely that I wanted to be an artist when I grew up.

I also met my lifelong best friend when I was eight. Over the years, every time we got together, we played role-playing games, which in those days consisted of reading books you liked, maybe making some costumes, and then going outside and pretending with all your imagination that you were someone else. We specialized in the Pony Express, the French and Indian War, and the Civil War—we were always reading the sort of books that listed "other books boys will enjoy" on the back flap. We each had a male alter ego/"secret identity" we used when playing pretend, because we were all too aware that boys had all the fun in the books we read. (We also sewed for and played very happily with dolls, but the dolls frequently had hair-raising adventures.) My parents never made any attempt to interfere with what I read; probably they were just glad that I liked to read.

When I was very young my father had a telescope out in the backyard; on summer evenings we used to go out and look at the moon and planets through it. That was probably the beginning of my fascination with space, and eventually with science fiction. I still remember the haunting paintings by Chesley Bonestall in a *Life* magazine feature on space back in the Fifties. (I learned the meaning of the word "hypothetical" from one of the captions: "a double star viewed from a hypothetical planet." I was crushed to learn that "hypothetical" meant "imaginary"; that the planet, with its stunning crags and craters, orbiting that mysterious double sun wasn't real.) When I was six my parents took me on a vacation to New York state. By far my most vivid memories of the trip are still of the Hayden Planetarium at the Museum of Natural History. (It still looks just as I remember it.)

Most people who are going to become science-fiction readers seem to stumble on the genre when they're fairly young; usually between the ages of eight and fourteen. I suspect that this is because science fiction is often filled with unfamiliar terminology. It's easier for children, who find a lot of things confusing or unfamiliar, to accept that they won't understand everything they read. An adult has a harder time being patient with a book filled with strange concepts. Andre Norton novels and the Robert Heinlein juveniles seem to be the books that get most science-fiction fans addicted.

◆ *Joan D. Vinge*

I was always fascinated by Sputnik and astronauts and news about "new discoveries" like transistors and lasers, but I didn't know science fiction existed until I was in ninth grade; barely within the "window." By then I had already picked up the message that girls weren't supposed to be interested in science or math, and I had begun to avoid them as subjects in school.

Then one day, looking through the book rack at the local grocery store, I found Andre Norton's book *Storm over Warlock*. I liked the hero's picture on the cover, and although I had no idea what a "Terran Survey Team" was (I was afraid "Terrans" would turn out to be some sort of weird aliens), I decided to try it. It changed my life. It turned my head around. It took me on the most wonderful trip to somewhere else I'd ever experienced. Finally I realized that a way existed to get back to that "hypothetical planet" beneath its strange, haunting sky; that writers existed who actually seemed to believe someday we might all get there. Andre Norton started me reading science fiction, and although I never suspected it at the time, her writing would directly or indirectly influence almost every major life choice I made from then on.

After that, I gave up reading about horses (though not drawing or riding them) and read almost nothing but science fiction. Science fiction helped me remain sane during high school (just like a lot of other people) by releasing me from the miseries of high school's rigid peer structure and the stifling early Sixties. I was tall, intellectual, and painfully shy—born to be part of the nerd pack. But, like a lot of other science-fiction fans, I learned through reading science fiction that The Way

Things Were was not necessarily The Way Things Had to Be. It was probably the most important lesson I learned in school. If I ever need reassurance that writers can have an effect on the lives of their readers, I have only to think about my own experience.

For some reason, I didn't try very often to draw or paint other worlds, although art was still my main compulsion. But I continued to experiment with writing stories, and the stories I wrote were suddenly all science fiction. Most writers of science fiction get their start that way; you have to love reading the stuff, to begin with, or you are unlikely to want to write it. But I did what a lot of science fiction fans apparently do: I began things and never finished them; tossed them into a drawer when I got stuck, maybe taking them out later but usually just starting something new and not finishing that. I often wrote late at night, when I was supposed to be sleeping, by the dim glow of the television set in my room so that my mother wouldn't realize I was still up. Writing was my very private hobby in high school; I rarely showed my stories to anyone, even my friends. Art and poetry were my "serious" creative outlets.

Then I went to college, intending to major in art and become a commercial artist. I ran afoul of the kind of people who often wind up teaching art at state schools—artists who were only there because they couldn't make a living from their art, and lacked the sensitivity of a real teacher. Three semesters was enough to destroy my "restless urge to draw" completely. I went on through a series of other majors, including English, finally graduating with a degree in anthropology/archeology . . . thanks to my continuing interest in science fiction.

Andre Norton was not only responsible for my interest in science fiction, but in anthropology as well. Her book *The Time Traders* had recreated Northern Europe in about 2000 B.C. so vividly that I had been haunted by it for years, the way I had once been haunted by a hypothetical planet. I finally realized that regular history courses would never get me there, and signed up for a European prehistory course. (I actually hoped, for the first and only time, that I would have to do a term paper.) I did my term paper on the Beaker Folk from Norton's novel. And, much to my surprise, I discovered that anthropology affected me the way science fiction did: it turned my head around, made me wonder "where has anthropology been . . . ?" I'd always enjoyed reading fantasy as well as science fiction (when I refer to "science fiction" I mentally include fantasy, just as they do at the bookstore), and anthropology seemed to set off the same kind of excitement in me. My motto became, "Archeology is the anthropology of the past, and science fiction is the anthropology of the future."

"Broadening" is a word that I am generally reluctant to use, but it's the only one I know of that expresses the thing I find appealing about both science fiction and anthropology: they prove to me over and over again that the way I live life in twentieth-century America is not the only way there is; that people in other places and times on Earth (and probably off of it) have dealt with the universe and its perversities in very different ways, many of which work equally well. A B.A. in anthropology is not generally a terribly useful degree

(I had originally planned on getting a Ph.D.), but I have found it to be extremely useful in my writing. Not only did it teach me to look at human behavior from a fresh perspective, with a kind of parallax view, but it also gave me the ethnographer's structural tools for creating imaginary societies, for building worlds that I wanted to write about. It has also given me a rich mine of real-world cultures and myths to mix and match when I'm creating new worlds. I generally write what has been called "world-building" fiction, a branch of the field that has grown as more social-science-trained writers have broadened the science base in "science fiction."

I was in college in the late Sixties, a time that seemed to be very much in sync with the world view I'd started to form from reading science fiction, specifically Andre Norton's work. My support of the peace, ecology, and equal-rights movements grew naturally out of the values I'd found in her books, and the kind of person that reading them had made me want to become. These values also inspired my support of one more thing— the women's movement. Way back in junior high school I'd discovered that "Andre" Norton was actually a woman, and it had made a deep impression on me. It did not immediately suggest to me that I could grow up to be a science-fiction writer myself, but it made her more real—and somehow more wonderful—to me. In the early mid-Sixties, well before the women's movement became widespread, I read her *Ordeal in Otherwhere*, the first book I'd ever read with an honest-to-God liberated woman as the protagonist. Not only were female protagonists extremely unusual at the time, but this character came from a world on which sexual equality was the norm. I never forgot that, and in the late Sixties, when I began to see articles on feminism, something fell into place for me in a very profound way.

A great deal of the science fiction I read while growing up was *not* socially progressive or forward looking, even if it was high tech. Science fiction has historically had a reputation for sociopolitical conservatism that is not unjustified. It didn't bother me much at the time. I accepted the party line; I was still young, and so caught up in the "forest" of cultural norms that I couldn't see "trees" such as sexism. The exotic locales and strange customs (as far as they went) of science fiction still offered me escape from my limited visibility, and the few writers like Norton were a breath of fresh air. But I remember reading Heinlein's *Podkayne of Mars* only a few months before I read my first article on feminism (in the *Saturday Review*), and thinking with a sigh that "I would never be as feminine as Podkayne. . . ."

A few months later I read that article, and then more like it. And it struck me at last that *I* wasn't the one with the problem—Podkayne was. There was more than one way to look at the relationship between the sexes, and what was good and bad, valid or invalid, about it. I experienced a great deal of anger then, but more than that a feeling of pride, and a sense of profound relief. I realized that I didn't have to pretend to be a man in fantasies to do all the things I wanted to do; and that it wasn't my fault, or my failure, if I didn't wear the straitjacket of "femininity" gracefully. I still wanted to marry and have a family, but I also wanted a career, and the support of a man who wanted an equal partner, not a five-foot, ten-inch "little woman."

But at that point I still felt no ambition to become a published writer. Despite my "restless urge," I was afraid to show my work around seriously, for fear of getting my creativity crushed the way I had with my art. I had begun to understand that I had an inborn need to create something; I was afraid that if my urge, which had already been transferred from art to writing, was beaten down again, there would be no outlet left for it.

But then I met my first husband, Vernor Vinge, who was already a published science-fiction writer (another way in which Andre Norton and science fiction changed my life). He gave me the encouragement I needed to work seriously on a story and send it out. I actually sold the story ("Tin Soldier"), and after that there was no turning back. My career had found me. (It is possible to take quite a bit of rejection without losing courage once you have actually sold a story.)

When I look back at the odd course that led me to become a writer, there is really no way I could have predicted the outcome. But having become a writer, I have given thought over the years to the things that have shaped and affected my work. In the beginning it was only the "restless urge," the blind, instinctive need to create something, and a fascination with the strange that was science fiction, that drove me to write. But as I continued to work, and saw that my writing was not a fluke, I realized there were other forces, both conscious and unconscious, influencing everything I did.

I still write primarily for myself, and I find it difficult if not impossible to work on a story I'm not completely interested in. But beyond that, I am unquestionably affected by what is going on around me, whether I like it or not. The peace or chaos in my personal life affects the lightness or darkness of my prose; the sociopolitical climate affects how I regard my characters' actions (because science fiction is really about the present, no matter how much we try to pretend that it is about the past or future); music and images inspire me constantly, striking directly the creative, nonverbal part of my brain where story ideas take form; and other writers' works suggest new areas I want to explore myself (when I have the time to read them).

The response of readers and/or critics has an influence, for better or worse, on what I write, as well; although generally I prefer to work with an editor I trust, and disregard other critics as much as is humanly possible. I believe a writer's work can be considerably strengthened by the input of a knowledgeable editor; it is too easy to become so close to your own work that you can't see it clearly. But for input to be meaningful, it must come from someone with whom the writer shares a bond of mutual respect and creative vision; preferably it should occur before the book or story is published, since criticism after the fact is, for the most part, moot.

Science fiction is a unique field in that the writers actually have an opportunity to meet their fans and editors (and critics) face to face, at the numerous science-fiction conventions that are held around the country. The feedback is generally gratifying, and it can affect what a writer works on subsequently as well—if everybody, including the publisher, wants "the next book about so-and-so," sometimes the temptation to write it becomes overwhelming. I find myself writing a lot of sequels lately, and knowing that there is a ready audience for them helps when you're concerned with making a living—a consideration all professionals have to keep in mind. I have also found that, as a mother with two small children, new and unique ideas do not come to my mind as easily as they used to, so I am grateful to have "future histories" that I'm already familiar with, and characters that I already know and like, to give me a springboard to new books.

But the bottom line still remains the same: if the actual idea for the book leaves me cold, I will not be able to write it. Each book has to have its own reason for being, and its own integrity in my own mind, or else I might as well not write it. I am easily blocked as a writer and lack of interest in a subject is one of the surest ways I know of to keep me from getting something done. (I am not a fast writer anyway; I have found that I am able to supplement my income by doing movie novelizations, which I *can* do quickly, and even have some fun with.)

Although in the beginning and end I am writing for myself as my own "ideal audience," I am also aware that I'm writing to a real audience, and imagine—or hope—that I am having some effect on them, as Andre Norton and science fiction generally had on me. I choose to write science fiction instead of mainstream fiction because I enjoy the freedom the field gives me to experiment. Good characters are extremely important to me when I read, and also when I write; there was a time when I almost stopped reading science fiction (which happens to a lot of people somewhere around college age) because so much of it was poorly written, with cardboard characters pushed around the landscape simply to make the plot go. My first husband told me that the point was to read for the ideas, so I tried to do that; but in time I realized the two things did not have to be mutually exclusive.

And yet I also realized that it *was* the ideas I loved about science fiction, as opposed to mainstream fiction. Taking characters I am interested in getting to know, putting them into strange and different situations, allowing them (and the reader) to discover something about human nature and their own individual natures—to see what the story teaches me, along with my characters—is more satisfying and gives me more pleasure than anything I know.

But at the same time I can't help being aware of the potential I have for teaching my readers certain things. Feminism, which for me is more a specific kind of humanism, is an inescapable part of my world view and my writing. I try not to preach when I write, for writers who set out primarily to preach quickly end up preaching only to the converted. I think of myself basically as an entertainer, and embrace the philosophy that "a spoonful of suger helps the medicine go down." Andre Norton served as a profound role model for me while entertaining me endlessly with the humanity and variety of her characters and stories; I hope that I may have the same sort of effect on at least a few of my readers. I attempt to let my characters speak for themselves, letting them interact and butt heads and learn—along with the reader, I hope—and through my characters I try not only to make female readers more aware of the possibilities open to them in their lives, but make male readers see that strong, competent women and sensitive, thoughtful men are not anathema. If a man can read a satisfying science-fiction novel in which "liberated" characters appear, and enjoy it anyway, it is my hope (and it has been borne out occasionally) that the experience might lessen the reader's fear of meeting similar people in the real world.

I have never found it more difficult to write about male characters than female characters; I try to respect my characters' individual integrity, just as I would if they were people I met in the real world. In fact, being able to "play God" and create characters who answer to me, I am able to write about a higher percentage of men who are the kind of man I would like to know than I might actually encounter in the real world.

If anything, I sometimes feel that I have more difficulty writing successfully about women characters, simply because I am more aware of them as role models, and have to fight against the urge to keep them on their good behavior when they honestly and realistically should be covering as much of the spectrum of good and evil as any man. (I think women may have an easier time "getting into the heads" of male characters than vice versa because historically women, as an underclass, have been forced to know what was on a man's mind almost before he did, or suffer for it. Men, on the other hand, had less reason to understand "what it is women want," because to understand is to sympathize, which makes continued exploitation difficult. And on a personal level, having done so much "boy's book" role-playing as a girl, it has never been hard for me to "pretend" I was seeing things through the eyes of a male character when I write. It's all part of the "speculative fiction.")

I do not think of my writing style as being specifically "female" as opposed to "male," however. I used to be aware of what I thought of as "male" and "female" prose styles while reading science fiction when I was in college; the characteristic styles, however, were not invariably linked to writers of the appropriate sex. (At the time I thought of Le Guin as having a "male" style because her prose was spare and straightforward; I did not think of Norton's style as specifically either male or female.) Over the years I have come to feel that such distinctions are largely artificial, and that they tend to become less pronounced as male and female stereotypes break down. In any case, I feel that a well-written work will transcend such basically stereotypical categories.

In the same way, the treatment of women characters as peculiar, incomprehensible, or less than human in a lot of "classic" works of Golden Age science fiction seems to me to be a result of stereotypical attitudes (on the part of both male and female writers), prejudices of the sort I blindly accepted during much of my life. Occasionally I deal in my stories with characters who regard women that way (since such people are still at large in my universe, and I expect they always will be), but I write from the position that such an attitude is bigoted or blind, and hope that my readers (if not always my characters) will reach the same conclusion.

I have often felt fortunate that I work in the science-fiction field, because the field has proved to be far more open to the kind of points I want to make with my work than most of society is. The science-fiction field was, for a long time, a particular stronghold of male chauvinism, but I entered it during a period of general social change, when some of the groundwork of opening up the field to women writing as women (and not forced to hide their light behind male or androgynous names) had been done by other women, writers like Ursula Le Guin, Joanna Russ, and Anne McCaffrey. There was a period in the mid-Seventies when women were a novelty act (my friend joked about the all-women issue of *Analog* in which I had a story, calling it "Joan D. Vinge and Her All-Girl Band"). But because of the ongoing changes in the field, I experienced an almost utopian atmosphere of acceptance for my work. I believed that if readers were exposed to stories by women writers, even in all-women anthologies, the quality of the work would be recognized, and the "freakish" aspect would quickly fade; and that was basically what happened. I was fortunate, and I was not alone, because many other women began writing science fiction during that same period.

I believed that if women were given an honest chance to show how well they wrote, they would gain real acceptance; and through the Seventies and into the Eighties that appeared to happen. I was proud of the people in the field for proving that they were not only on the cutting edge of progress technologically, but also socially—that they believed just as strongly in social change. In interviews I was often asked why so many women had started writing science fiction all at once, and my answer was that feminism had made the real difference, making those women who had always been readers stop and say, "If I want to do that, I can." It was true for me, and every woman writer I knew considered herself to be a feminist. (So did many of the new male writers; and even the most hidebound of the older male authors actually seemed to be making some effort to raise their consciousnesses—with mixed results.) I think that women who had always been receptive to science fiction were particularly likely to be open to feminism as well; because we already had the ability to accept a new and different perspective on life.

There was a time when I would have ended an essay like this here, on an uplifting and positive note that reflected my pride at being a part of a field where I am free to realize my human potential to the fullest, without limitations or penalties. Unfortunately, as I remarked before, science fiction does not reflect the future so much as it reflects the present. My husband tells me of conversations on the train not just with men but with businesswomen for whom feminists are "some bunch of lesbians and weirdos"; who express surprise when he tells them that their goals are feminist goals, or that they wouldn't be riding that train, briefcases clutched in their hands, if their (older) sisters hadn't fought for their right to do it.

Our society has gone through a period of major backsliding after the social progress of the Sixties and

Seventies; and this has been reflected in the science-fiction field. Jeanne Gomoll, a reader and fan who has written a great deal on feminism and science fiction, recently published an article detailing the move by certain (male) critics within the field to deny and belittle the work of the "world-building," humanist/feminist writers of the Seventies as inferior and/or aberrant. The trend depresses me, but it does not surprise me, any more than it changes my attitudes or goals. It only reflects what I have experienced in my own life; that reality is more complicated and ultimately more disappointing than our dreams. Trying to continue a writing career and raise a family *is* more difficult for a woman than for a man. Although my husband is both an editor in the field and an avowed feminist, still I am the one on whom most of the family responsibilities fall, which is not the case with most of the male writers I know. (Most of the women writers I know are not married, although a few are, and now have babies and conflicts of their own.)

But all that does not change the genuine progress that women have made in and out of the field; we have won a foothold in science fiction as well as in the real world, and we are not about to give it up. And it does not change a very personal truth for me: however much I treasure my children and my family life (and I honestly do not regret the ways in which children have limited certain aspects of my career, because they have enriched my life so much, both as a human being and as a writer), if I could not fulfill my *need* to write, my restless urge, I would lose myself. My work is my soul;

125

is what I do for *me* and no one else. Self-expression
is a need that is as vital for a woman as it is for a man.
And now I believe more strongly than ever in the potential that science fiction has for opening minds and
spirits, in the importance of its writers continuing to
serve up a little healthy humanity in a "spoonful of
sugar."

It is, quite honestly, something of a surprise to me
to find myself at this point in ending my essay—realizing that I am not so much writing a kind of memoir
as a cautionary tale. But experience has proven for me
the saying, "The price of freedom is eternal vigilance."
And that old feminists never die; they just say, "Write
On. . . ."

Biographical Notes

Born in Baltimore, Maryland, Joan Vinge has been writing
since junior high school. She attended San Diego State University and received a B.A. in anthropology. Joan has worked
as a salvage anthropologist, and her strong science background has helped shape and influence her writings. She has
won Hugo awards for the novelette "Eyes of Amber" (1978)
and the novel *The Snow Queen* (1981). She currently resides
in upstate New York with her husband, editor/publisher
James R. Frenkel.

Books by Joan D. Vinge

Catspaw (Warner, 1988)

Ladyhawke (New American Library, 1985)

Phoenix in the Ashes (Bluejay Books, 1985)

World's End (Bluejay Books, 1984)

Psion (Delacorte Press, 1982)

The Snow Queen (Dial, 1980)

Eyes of Amber and Other Stories (New American Library, 1979)

Fireship (Dell Publishing Co., 1978)

The Crystal Ship (T. Nelson, 1976)

THE WRITER AS NOMAD

Pamela Sargent

Not long ago, I was asked to write an introduction to a second collection of my short fiction. Unable to think of anything to say about the stories themselves, I ended up writing about how, for years, even after the publication of a few stories, I couldn't really acknowledge that I was a writer at all. Left unwritten was the explanation of *why* I felt that way. Like the well-bred hostess of a dinner party, I did not want to invite readers to meet my guests, the stories, while bombarding them with too much unsuitable talk. I joked a little, made a few darker remarks, and left a lot of things unsaid.

I did not, in the beginning, choose writing as a profession. Writing was, for me, something I had to do to survive—not economically, but psychologically.

Writing was a compulsion, a way to make sense, met-
aphorically, of various events, to find a purpose in my
life, and even, at times, to escape it. One might say
that the stories were game to be hunted and tracked,
brought down, and then eaten. Publication, like the
mounted heads on a hunter's walls, was merely a by-
product of the pursuit, one that was not really essential; the act of writing and the mental nourishment
gained from that act seemed far more important. Writing was a way of living.

I was, in fact, a kind of nomad, keeping my distance
from communities where everything is fixed and settled. There's something to be said for being physically
nomadic. I felt most free when everything I owned
could fit into a couple of suitcases and a small trunk;
this meant I had less to lose, and could always escape.
But what I want to consider here is the psychological
nomad, which is what many writers are and what science-fiction and fantasy writers in particular may be.

At our best, we're trying to seek out new trails and
find new game; we see more familiar literary hunting
grounds as overhunted. We learn the skills we need
from other hunters who keep nearer to their home
ground, then move toward unknown lands and hope
that some of our tribe will follow. We want a different
kind of nourishment, and may also be trying to escape
the tribal customs that constrict the movements of
many of us.

During my teens, when some of my contemporaries
were wrestling with such problems as grades, high school
cliques, dates, or preparing for the PSATs, I was deliv-

ered into the hands of an institution in the hope that it might keep me from destroying myself. By then, I had two suicide attempts and various other attempts at escape to my credit; my family no longer knew what to do with me.

During the months I was in this place, which was supposedly designed to help me, I learned how to appease one of my keepers with cigarettes, money, and some personal possessions so that she would not report my transgressions to her superiors. I learned how to tell those in authority what they wanted to hear and how to conceal the truth; I have distrusted such people ever since. I endured the assaults of one man, and didn't report them, although that wasn't out of any misplaced concern for him. Either I wouldn't have been believed, and would have had the additional problem of reprisals on his part, or I *would* have been believed, in which case I would be blamed for allowing the assaults to happen and would only lose what little freedom I had.

This sage advice on how to deal with my problem was offered by my friend Gwen, a ghetto kid who knew her way around such institutions and considered this place a paradise compared to the one she had been in earlier. She also gave me a few pointers on how to defend myself in fights, tips that did come in handy.

Some of my other friends were Lydia, whose parents had decided that she needed to be whipped into shape when they discovered she was a lesbian; Raul, an angry young man who had suffered abuse as a child and whom I planned to marry if we could get away and manage to lie about our ages; and Bob, a boy who had occasional blackouts after which he couldn't recall what he had done, but who struck me as one of the gentlest people I had known. My ability to predict a friend's actions was obviously impaired; little more than a year later, Bob was in prison doing time for a murder he couldn't remember having committed.

None of us had any ambitions for the future other than getting out, and couldn't really imagine what would happen to us after that. Bob had a fantasy of running away and finding a house where we could all hide out, but those plans never came to fruition; it was easier to dream about it. Our favorite recreational activity was washing down some of the tranquilizers and psychotropic drugs used to keep us malleable with large swigs of whiskey a bribed adult would smuggle onto the grounds. This wasn't hard to do; we pretended to swallow our drugs, spat them out, and saved them for later. We could escape for a little while by blotting out all thought.

The solace of writing, of struggling to recast some of my experiences into fictional form in order to make sense of them, or to create the refuge of an entirely imaginary world, was taken away from me. I had to learn how to face reality, my keepers reasoned; therefore, my writing, in which the imagined could take on a kind of reality, had to be discouraged. Clearly, it hadn't helped me before (so they believed), and wasn't likely to aid my adjustment now; I dimly felt that writing was considered somehow dangerous.

I did, however, find a tool to help me in my mental wandering. Someone had left an old, beat-up paperback lying around, a copy of Alfred Bester's *The Stars My Destination*. This story of the tormented Gully Foyle, who was able to "jaunt," or teleport, himself from one place to another, immediately spoke to me.

That paperback became one of my treasures; I kept it with me most of the time so that it wouldn't be stolen. I was well aware that I couldn't teleport myself out of the institution, but did begin to imagine a future self, the adult Pamela Sargent who had finally escaped. I visited this self in my mind and saw myself looking back, free at last, safely distant and able to look back with some objectivity. Whenever I was enduring a painful or humiliating experience, or a dark, despairing mood, I tried to jaunt or migrate mentally past that time.

I also told myself that, some day, I would draw on what had happened to me in my writing, find a way to make order and sense of it, find a purpose in what would otherwise be only meaningless, brutal, or random acts. I would gain some freedom inside myself, if nowhere else. It didn't occur to me then that my situation, in an exaggerated way, reflected some experiences common to other girls and women.

I have to consider myself lucky in the end. I returned to a school where a few fine teachers encouraged my intellectual ability, which must have seemed latent at best. I won a scholarship to college and, later, became reconciled with those who I thought had abandoned me earlier.

But for a long time, I was also careful not to get too close to anyone. Close relationships, I believed, would almost inevitably lead to either betrayal or violent confrontations; they meant giving someone else power over oneself. Under the guise of friendship, love, or concern, others could inflict a great number of wounds. I was scarred enough; I was going to travel light.

I continued to write from time to time; the solitude of writing was appealing. But for the most part, I hunted alone, and kept my distance from the rest of the tribe.

Often, I threw away my stories after they were written. Part of this was a natural fear of criticism, or insecurity about having the stories read and judged by others. But I also feared revealing too much of myself to anyone else; the most meaningful stories were the ones I kept hidden.

I ate my game by myself, and didn't think of sharing it with anyone else. Writing was my private act of rebellion, and I had seen what could happen when you rebelled too openly; writing was my refuge, one I might lose if it were revealed. Maybe I should have learned, through my experience with *The Stars My Destination* earlier, that writing could also be a lifeline to others.

During my senior year in college, I managed, to my surprise, to sell a story. This was unintentional; I'd been encouraged to submit it by two aspiring writers I knew, but had not expected that it would be bought. There was some satisfaction in actually getting a check for this small act of rebellion, but also a fear that future game might now evade me.

I reached a compromise, one that would allow me to keep writing while protecting my refuge. I wrote, but did not concern myself with what happened to the stories after they were published; I shared some of my game, but didn't want to hear other people's opinions of it. I put published stories on my shelves, but did not think of myself as a "real" writer.

I kept to my own trails. I stayed away from writers' workshops and other such gatherings, regarding them much the way a hunter would view chattering companions; they might frighten away whatever I was tracking. Gradually, I came to see that a good editor might lead me to a trail or hunting ground I otherwise wouldn't have explored; other writers could suggest new methods for trapping or bringing down my game. Writing remained a solitary pursuit, but there could be companionship after the hunt.

Writing became a way of communicating with others. Given the masks I had learned to hide behind much of the time, it was virtually the only way I had of doing so.

I was extremely fortunate to be doing my early writing at a time when the women's movement was growing, although I didn't see that in the beginning. The early complaints of feminists seemed strange to me at first. Didn't they understand that some things couldn't be changed, and that all we could do was to survive or escape in whatever small ways were open to us? The prospect of exposing oneself in sessions of consciousness-raising seemed repellent and threatening; the notion that others might once again tell me what I should think and feel was disturbing. I had found a way to shield myself and did not want to lose it.

It was the writing of feminists that brought about my change of heart and made me see that I did indeed have a bond with other women. In their work and their

THE WRITER AS NOMAD ◆

lives, I came to see, there were other choices besides
either surrendering or retreating. I had believed that I
had escaped; in fact, I had only imprisoned myself.

Other women were hunting; some of them were
following the trails of science fiction and fantasy. The
best fantastic literature and the most profound feminism have this in common: they are subversive, continually challenging the accepted wisdom of the tribe
while seeking change and a new way of understanding
and viewing the world. They question, and probe, asking why things are as they are and looking for ways in
which they might be different.

I had dreamed of a future self able to look back at
the past with some understanding. In a sense, science
fiction involves a search for other future selves, imagined people who will look back on our present and near-
future as their past, perhaps seeing what we cannot and
showing us that there are paths out of the prisons our
age has built for us all.

Women writers of science fiction and fantasy encouraged me, by their example, to range farther afield.
Some of them were exploring territory other writers
had avoided. Their stories and novels raised questions,
illuminated some darker corners, expressed a rage I had
felt but had learned to suppress, pointed the way to
new possibilities, or entertained while poking fun at
some of our tribal ways. The game they had successfully hunted nourished me.

I began to assemble some of these stories in the
hope of putting together an anthology. If writing can
be seen as hunting, then editing a collection of stories

might be seen as gathering (or, perhaps uncharitably, as scavenging). These stories had fed me, and now I wanted to share them with others.

For a while, however, as I went from one publishing house to another with my proposal, I felt that no one wanted to accept this book. Some editors responded out of ignorance; could there actually be enough science fiction stories by women to fill a book? Others were skeptical or hostile, no doubt trying to protect the tribe from contamination. Still others thought it was a fine idea, but did not want to be the first to accept the morsels I offered.

My anthology, *Women of Wonder*, eventually did see print, along with two successive collections of science fiction by women, and now the trails those writers made have become clearly defined paths. I had done no more than gather the food to which those writers had guided me, and lead others to their tracks; but working on those books gave me more faith in my own writing. I like to think of *Women of Wonder* as a book that the frightened teenager clutching her copy of *The Stars My Destination* would have enjoyed reading.

It may be that a lot of my own writing, in some way, is for that girl as well. Much of my work, and not just the books ostensibly published for young adults, is filled with people in their teens, many of whom are outsiders or outcasts from their tribes, who often *want* to be like everyone else and feel that their inability to fit in is a defect. In *Watchstar*, my protagonist, Daiya, is a girl preparing for her "ordeal," the rite of passage all young people in her telepathic village must endure, in which they are cut off from their community entirely and must confront their fears—fears that are given form and substance by the mental powers these people possess. In this society, people must conform, since even their thoughts can harm someone else. Daiya, with her questions and doubts, cannot fit in, and fails her ordeal; she becomes an outcast, yet cannot give up the ties she feels with her people.

My characters often wander quite a bit. In *Earthseed*, my first novel for young adults, my teenaged characters roam inside a hollowed-out asteroid that is itself a ship wandering through space, looking for a planet where the young people can settle. The cybernetic mind of this ship is the only parent they have ever known, and the only source of information about an Earth they've never seen. But much has been withheld from the ship's mind; gradually, the young people discover that a lot of what they've been told is either misleading or a lie. They are forced to confront their own weaknesses and to overcome them before they can leave their ship.

In my novel *The Shore of Women*, I chose to write about a world where women live in vast, walled cities, while men roam the wilderness outside and follow the life of hunters and gatherers. A nuclear war is in these people's past, and women are determined that men will never again acquire the means to wage such a war; women control all technology and teach the men to worship them as divine beings. My central characters are Birana, a young woman unjustly expelled from her city, and Arvil, a young man and a hunter who helps her to survive. The two begin to seek a refuge where they can be safe, but also have to overcome their most deeply felt beliefs in order to reach out to each other.

137

This story, however, is not theirs alone, but also that of Laissa, a young woman who begins to question her city's ways. Laissa's wandering is through historical records and archives, while the chronicle she eventually writes becomes a blow leveled at her society's assumptions.

No doubt my own experience is reflected in these tales, as well as in others. Yet these apparently recurring themes are not something I care to speculate about too much for fear of scaring off whatever stories my mind might be tracking now. I would not want to limit myself to only certain trails.

All of us who write are nomads and hunters, at least for a while. There are, however, traps for us as well.

We might find a well-traveled trail and decide to keep to it, instead of looking for new grounds. Some of us are tempted to settle near a likely grazing ground and to hunt the same herd over and over, preferring the safety of the familiar to the risks of new territory. Some of us domesticate our game, or stay in one place, tilling the soil and harvesting the same plants until the ground we work can yield no more. A lot of us see that even if we pursue the hunt, it's less frightening to join a band or tribe led by one explorer, and to share his game instead of seeking our own.

Too many of us fall into such traps, and there are plenty of people preparing them for us—readers who want us to stay in familiar lands without finding anything new there; editors who want to appease both their tribal chieftains and the rest of the tribe; critics who believe we belong in a particular territory and nowhere else; and writers who cling to the security of being among a like-minded clan or group instead of realizing that companionship can come only after a hunt that must be made alone. This desire for security and the settled life seems contrary to what working in science fiction and fantasy can offer us—new ideas, a different and illuminating perspective, a means to depict imaginatively the changes that may alter what we are or underline the truths about our nature, a method of heightening the familiar and making it seem very strange indeed.

Even when a writer explores new territory, without familiar trails, there are other risks. You might expend more energy in the hunt than the game can possibly yield. You may find nothing you can use. You may bring back your capture and see the tribe refuse it. If you write for a living, as I do, you learn that you have to roam over a greater area in order to avoid the traps, and cannot afford the luxury of pursuing only one kind of prey. You learn when to wait, when to strike, when to abandon one story when a more likely prospect suddenly presents itself, and how to find your way back to the story you had to leave. Small wonder that so many writers, after taking the trouble of laying down a path to new lands, decide they'd rather keep to it instead of moving on.

The need for hunting and gathering is an integral part of us; that is the life we led for most of our history. It's a life that, barring any future catastrophe, we are unlikely to regain. But we can hunt and gather among the arts, sciences, history, and human minds our society has formed.

Science fiction and fantasy at their best recognize this need, giving us a way to wander to new lands and then to return and share what we have found before we have to go hunting once more. At their worst, they provide a bare subsistence, hunt the same herds until they are decimated, or offer the tribe a drug to keep it tranquil. Such writing dulls the tribe, leaving it without nourishment, illumination, or hope—much like the earlier version of myself I mentioned before, the one for whom I try to write now.

Writing the kind of work many choose to label as science fiction or fantasy has given me the chance to roam and to find mental sustenance. Publishing it has enabled me to share what I've found with others. This is territory I may leave at some point—labels are another way of fencing ourselves in—but one that remains so vast that I'm likely to return to it.

Lately, I have been on the trail of those fascinating nomads, the Mongols, who, in their search for unity and order among themselves, safety from enemies, and more food and pasture land, ended up conquering most of the known world; this search is yielding some game in the form of a novel. I can't say where my writing will lead me in the future, only that I have to follow wherever the tracks I find lead me.

Biographical Notes

Pamela Sargent was born in Ithaca, New York, and attended the State University of New York at Binghamton, where she received a B.A. and an M.A. in philosophy. After holding various jobs, Pamela sold her first story in 1970; since then, she has become a prolific writer and editor. Her stories have appeared in *The Magazine of Fantasy and Science Fiction*, *Universe*, and *Fellowship of the Stars*, among other magazines and anthologies.

Pamela's *Women of Wonder* anthologies are important milestones in science fiction and fantasy. These anthologies directly confront issues important to women and their roles in society through the voices of the women writers. Pamela currently resides in upstate New York.

Books by Pamela Sargent

Venus of Shadows (Doubleday Foundation, 1988)

Alien Child (Harper & Row, 1988)

The Best of Pamela Sargent (Chicago, 1987)

Afterlives, with Ian Watson (Vintage Books, 1986)

The Shore of Women (Crown, 1986)

Venus of Dreams (Bantam Spectra Books, 1986)

Homesmind (Harper & Row, 1984)

Eye of the Comet (Harper & Row, 1984)

Earthseed (Harper & Row, 1983)

The Alien Upstairs (Doubleday, 1983)

The Golden Space (Simon & Schuster/Timescape Books, 1982)

Watchstar (Pocket Books, 1980)

The Sudden Star (Fawcett, 1979)

The New Women of Wonder (Vintage Books, 1978)

Starshadows (Ace Books, 1977)

Cloned Lives (Fawcett, 1976)

More Women of Wonder (Vintage Books, 1976)

Bio-Futures (Vintage Books, 1976)

Women of Wonder (Vintage Books, 1975)

NO-ROAD

Suzy McKee Charnas

ike most people, I started
out not knowing where I
was going; often I still don't know where I'm going,
but I have learned how I like to travel—on roads I make
for myself across uncharted territory; roads I make of
words.

Probably I was intended to be a visual artist, like
both my parents. But print won me, hands down.

I lived in a household with lots of books and grown-
ups who read them. Better yet, my parents read stories
out loud to me when I was little. And they made me
read stories out loud in turn to my kid sisters (is *The
Little Pond in the Woods* still out there someplace?),
no doubt to give the grown-ups a break at bedtime.

I suspect that having had stories lifted off the page
into spoken words for them when they were small in-

spired many in my generation to become authors. The transformation of those print marks into strings of words that make sense is an act of power children can readily recognize.

So it's no great wonder that I pestered my mother about reading to me until, in self-defense, she taught me to read one summer when I was still very young—to the annoyance next fall of my kindergarten teacher, who thought that was *her* job.

But Mom had already done it, and she'd done it well. She went over with me, in my own kid books, what the letters and letter combinations sounded like. Then she turned me loose on my own for as long as my patience, curiosity, and attention span held out.

In large part because of this experience, it is my belief that this country lost the literacy battle (maybe for good) when American public schools junked the phonetic method in favor of having kids memorize the appearance of individual words, an approach with a name as infantile as its content: the "look-say" method.

Word memorization is not only clumsy, slow, and dull, it is a subtle form of coercion that stifles completely the fun of learning to decode print.

As long as a child can read only memorized words, that child can read only what somebody else (the selector of the words on the memorization list) thinks a child ought to be able to read at his or her age (or maybe what anybody ought to be able to read at any age). In most schools, the child finds herself confined to some ghastly, gutless pap selected not for her actual interest or abilities but for the guarantee that the "ideas" con-

tained therein will not offend any so-called adult anywhere in the known universe.

The kid force-fed such stuff—*Fun with Dick and
Jane*, in my day—is not only bored to death but is in
chains and knows it. By the time she has doped out
the rules of phonics for herself, it's too late; the damage
is done. The whole process is tainted forever.

Whereas if you have been taught to make your way
through print armed with a sound system, you can, as
I did, pick up any book that intrigues you and root
around in it. Your freedom is bounded only by your
determination (useful in working out all the possible
soundings for a word like "roughneck,") and what your
busy little mind is *really* ready for, age be damned—
which is the level at which you end up reading anyway.

I tried the grown-up stuff, found it incomprehensible or silly, and settled down happily to read about
the concerns of people my own age and slightly older
in books written for those age levels.

Books were heaven. How not? In "real" life all adults
and most bigger kids are your masters when you are a
small kid. In stories, you can be master of anything
and anybody, including whole worlds that you never
dreamed existed.

Once you recognize that what is setting off this
private power trip is a string of words encoded by somebody else in marks on paper, and once you catch on to
the fact that, within the rough rules of how words relate
to each other, *you* are in control of the effects the words
make inside your mind—well, if you are at all suscep-
tible, you begin to want to write.

So you fool around trying to string together your own words on paper, to make your own stories happen over and over (and better and better) for yourself. When and if you become brave enough, you take a chance on your words unfolding your story in the mind of someone else: your first reader.

Stick with it and behold, you end up as the only kind of true magician that our fat, frightened culture recognizes (and that with more fear and contempt than true admiration): some sort of artist. A word artist, in fact. An author.

Terrific: what for?

I mean, *why* do it? To what purpose? You may not know for some time whether you *have* a purpose, beyond the exercise of the limited though perfectly respectable power to entertain (assuming you have that power).

I don't think I knew the "purpose" of my writing until my first novel, *Walk to the End of the World*, was published and several damned fools condemned me for having contaminated the sacred purity of science fiction with "feminist propaganda." I knew absolutely that I had not done anything of the sort and had no interest in doing it, but I was provoked into thinking about exactly what I *was* doing instead.

Something out of the ordinary certainly was going on, they were right about that part; nobody would call *Walk to the End of the World* "pure entertainment."

I found that for me the point of writing a book, as opposed to teaching a propaganda lesson, was to ask a question and find my way to some sort of satisfying answer—not necessarily *the* answer, assuming there is such a thing. And possibly, depending on the quality of the question, on the answer, and on individual readers, the point would be to suggest that the question itself was worth asking; worth a thinking person's attention and reflection as a question, not as the set of answers dictated by the conventional wisdom, or by any other party line.

Now you can see why I was accused of writing propaganda. This method inevitably raises certain issues that some people would prefer did not even exist. (In *Walk* the consideration was: what would a culture be like that carried sexism as we know it to its furthest extreme?) These are the folks who insist on one single known, fixed answer that everybody must subscribe to (which is effectively the same as making the question not exist).

To such people, the raising of any inquiry they don't like is seen as a provocative, aggressive, propagandistic act. In one very special sense this is true: it is propaganda, on behalf of using the brain for actual thinking rather than for exercising the drilled-in, knee-jerk responses of school, church, family, or party.

But is it propaganda in the other sense? No.

Here's how the question-asking process works for me—using a noncontroversial example, a book of mine called *The Vampire Tapestry.*

One winter I saw a couple of plays in New York about Dracula. The big Broadway period piece was an overrated bore, the little play at the Cherry Lane Theatre was funny and clever, and neither evening satisfied me. This is because what is intended as "pure" entertainment generally offers answers rather than questions so the audience can relax and enjoy itself—that is, not have to do any thinking.

Somewhere inside the idea of vampirism a really interesting question was crying to be let out, a question that, so far as I was aware, everybody had ignored or overlooked. I went looking for it, and I found it.

What if, I said to myself, the vampire were not a supernatural figure of Byronic romance and churchly paranoia but an animal in the same way that humans are animals, a product of the forces of evolution?

The original question yielded sub-questions: How could such a creature get along in modern America? What might he look like, how might he behave, what might we look like to him? Would he like the opera? What does he keep in his icebox? Some questions pointed the way to intriguing turns of plot, such as what goes on in the creature's head? Since I didn't know, in chapter three I sent him to a therapist and listened in.

I wrote until all the good questions were answered. And the original story, "The Ancient Mind at Work" (published first in *Omni* magazine), grew into a novel. Not a "vampire book," which would mean another serving of the same old traditional vampire answers, but a *novel*—in the sense of "new"—a novel whose protagonist happened to be a vampire.

I have been asked many times (to my intense gratification) if there will be a sequel. The answer is no; not unless, that is, a new question arises about my vampire to which I can't resist finding an answer.

Using the same questions again will not do. There's nothing so deadly as going over the same ground just to fill up another bunch of pages, your time, and your

bank account. You will also fill yourself up with boredom and your creativity will become stultified.

So where do new questions come from? Out of the
culture I live in, of course. The preoccupations of my
time are also my preoccupations. *Tapestry* is certainly
"about" predations of all kinds, as well as being a modern version of an ancient mythical figure.

How the general concerns of my culture arrive in
my head in the form of particular questions, I can't tell
you. I don't know. (Which is fine with me; sometimes
questions without answers turn out to be the best ones.)

Well, what about answers? Where do the answers
come from? Not from a plan, an outline, or a blueprint.
I don't write by forcing my characters over a set course
to a predetermined end. I don't read books written that
way, either. Unless done with real genius, a quality not
in lavish supply, such stories are as boring to read as
to write, because you can see from the start where the
author is taking you and pretty much how you're going
to be made to get there.

Frankly, a journey of several hundred pages isn't
worth the first step without surprises and mysteries
along the way; life is too short. And in the prefab novel
surprises and mysteries are as common as feathers on
hamsters.

I am the kind of writer I think of as "organic," as
in organic gardening. I plant my initial question and
then mooch around to see what I can coax into growing.
You could say that instead of building a story to dem-
onstrate the cleverness of my predrawn design, I grow
a story to discover the fruits—mostly unknown to me
at the start—implicit in the initial seed.

This process is in many ways a blind one, full of uncertainties. That's what draws me to it: the potentialities, which are what excited me about printed words in the first place.

On a more practical level, it takes me at least a year, more often two or three, to write a book, and I am not a patient person by nature. If I knew the answers to my questions too early, I'd be too bored to continue.

So to hold my interest (never mind yours), there has to be suspense. There have to be surprises and delights for *me*. If I do my job well, I have the added pleasure of passing these on so that the reader, too, can be surprised and delighted. Or horrified, or chastened, or exalted, or whatever happens.

Not, mind you, that I can honestly present myself as without sin in the realm of authorial tyranny. There have been times when I've seen clear answers from afar, and I've shooed my characters along in that direction (quickly, because once I "know" where it's all going, I get itchy to have the job over and done with so I can get on to something more interesting).

Disaster. Characters turn to chipboard. Every word drops leadenly onto the page and just lies there.

Salvation lies in backing off and letting the characters do and say whatever they want to. Eventually they relent and show me on the page the direction and the solutions that they've spun for, by, and among themselves, free from authorial chivvying.

That is the inner dynamic of writing for me: the tension between my author-ity (*I* thought up the questions and the characters, and my artistic judgment, my writing skills, my blah-blah-blah make me the *boss* here) and the integrity that the material itself develops as we go along.

Then there are fortuitous intrusions and gifts from the "real" world, like the headline "Slime Coated Men Arrested Near Millions" that showed up in the local paper one morning and irresistably muscled its way into my second young adult novel. Or the glimpse of a certain British explorer on television whose face I knew at once belonged in *Dorothea Dreams*. (His remembered image was the start of the character who became Ricky Maulders in that book.) That's part of the outer dynamic of my work.

So is my practice of giving out the penultimate draft to selected readers for criticism. These are people (not the same ones for every book) who have learned that when I say I want honest reactions I mean it; but at the same time that just because reader A says that my heroine would never do *that, that* will not automatically vanish from the finished version. Readers don't want that kind of responsibility and they're right to refuse it.

However if, say, three out of five such readers note that there is some kind of problem just at the point where my heroine does *that*, then chances are pretty good that I need to rethink *that* and find out what's wrong.

This feedback process is essential for me. I write a story in the first place to play with questions no one else has asked or answered to my satisfaction, so I write for myself in the deepest sense. It's crucial for me to make sure that I've communicated clearly enough with myself to be understood by eavesdroppers—readers.

I see myself as an experimenter, not in the sense of exploring avant-garde forms (I don't) but in something like a scientific sense. What I do in making a story has always seemed to me a lot like my understanding of Einstein's concept of a "thought experiment."

I formulate my questions and work out my answers without messing around in the real, physical world at all (except to the extent of putting real ink marks on real paper). So it's all in my head—and later, if I've done my work well (and find a publisher who does theirs), in your head. More or less.

A pretty chilly process, you might think; except that all the terms in my experiments are people—fictional people, yes, but it's the actions, words, and passions of the characters which serve as the forces and vectors of the experiment. My questions are the characters' dilemmas. For instance, how can Alldera, coming out of the most abject and horrific conditions of slavery, adapt to life among the free, nomadic Riding Women in *Motherlines? Can* she?

Which brings me to questions of character. Where do characters come from?

I know exactly what kicks each one off. There's no mystery about that. The two young men of *Walk to the End of the World* I took from a screen version of a romantic novel I had loved as a kid. Sheel, of *Motherlines*, grew from a young woman I saw in a crosstown bus in New York one summer day. I can see her now, sitting just behind the driver, facing me. She had blond hair and a long, graceful neck, and she wore a moss-green dress and sat with the shy composure of a painted Madonna.

Valentine, of the young adult novel *The Bronze King*, looks a lot like my younger sister at fourteen. Paavo Latvela, the wizard in that book, took shape as an amalgam of two performers I'd seen on stage, one an instrumentalist, the other a singer. Not surprising, since that book is about music as magic.

The start is always some physical quality—usually something I see, sometimes the voice, the bearing, the presence—of a real person. That's all I have to go on, since in general I don't know anything about the actual inner life of the person I am observing, certainly not enough to describe it accurately (even in the case of my sister. Maybe especially in the case of my sister).

We all do this kind of character creation every time we meet a new person and on the basis of what our senses first tell us, form some initial idea of what they are like, of their inner life. If we get to know them better, we begin to find out just how "fictionalizing" our early assessment was.

With characters in a story, the process is much the same. As they act and feel and speak on the page, I learn about their inner natures, modifying what I thought I knew about them when I began. The difference is that as a character comes into better focus, whatever fragment of reality I started with is adulterated with elements from half a lifetime of exposure to lots of other people, real and fictional. The character flows and shifts as it reveals, or maybe congeals, itself.

The wizard Paavo Latvela, for example, soon acquired certain speech mannerisms that had belonged to my Viennese grandmother. Sheel became not shy and composed like (maybe) the woman on the bus but a tough, aggressive, fundamentally "macha" warrior rather like an angry and combative student I had in a class I once taught.

So I can't say that I consciously develop characters in stories. I start with whatever bit of reality sets off a character in my mind, and then I try to keep up with the changes and revelations that follow—the surprises that keep me interested, the way surprises keep us interested in the real people we know.

Of course there has to be a coherent center that grounds a fictional person in something a reader will recognize as credibile, if not real. Where this work is done I don't know. It seems to do itself, using the facilities of some dark portion of my brain. That part is a mystery.

Why I write in and around the genre of fantasy and science fiction is not. In this genre I can use characters unusual enough to hold my interest without having to force them to fit "reality" as we like to think we know it. I am free to work with characters like Flynn, the survivor of Earth's death who narrates "Listening to Brahms," with the space pilot Dee Steinway of "Scorched Supper on New Niger," and her cat-companion Ripotee. Or with Floria Landauer, who does therapy with a creature of myth. Or the vampire, Weyland, himself.

Certainly some of these folks could appear in mainstream fiction, but the details of their lives would have to be worked out in terms of credit cards, terrorists, condos, cars, and cops. This notion appeals to me as much as having a shot of Novocaine in the frontal lobes, or watching a week of daytime television.

Dr. Weyland does in fact have to deal with the "real" world, but from the unique vantage point of being a vampire. This adds a twist, a quirky edge, to everything he experiences, and so makes his experience new. As a "realistic" character in mainstream fiction he would have to be just plain crazy. I would have wound up writing about his terrible childhood.

What interested me was his presence in our world as an alien being, not as another dreary fictional psychopath. He had to be a real vampire, not a pathetic, dangerous loon who thinks he's a vampire. Therefore the book had to be a fantasy.

Also, in fantasy you can fool around with matters that are not part of the received culture at large, without having to provide so much explanation and justification that you end up writing a textbook or a tract instead of a novel.

Take *Motherlines*, a book in which the question "What might a society of women without men be like?" is answered: "This all-woman society's members have become capable, as a group, of the full spread of human behavior including that portion that our present culture marks Men Only."

In that book I didn't have to *explain* such a revolutionary notion (and if you don't think it is revolutionary, look around you). A good thing, since I wasn't aware of this answer while I was writing. I started, it will be recalled, with the question. To find the answer I turned the Riding Women loose and recorded what happened. They created their answer in a direct way that would be simply impossible in a mainstream novel.

Surprise: feminism has just naturally reared its disruptive and unruly head again, so let me deal with that issue here.

Here is my capsule history of fantasy and science fiction: at first the boys wrote a lot of good and bad stuff for other boys to read, but except for a few, such as Theodore Sturgeon, they left vast areas of human experience relatively untouched—mostly what wasn't about wars, hierarchies, or toys but was about emotions, social flow, relationships—you know, *girl* stuff.

Which was nifty for women writers who came along in force in the Sixties and Seventies (I had the good fortune to be one of them) and found all this nearly (you should excuse the expression) virgin territory waiting to be explored. Now everybody's out there, which is exactly as it should be. Much of the genre is maturing as a consequence, which I chalk up to the influence of the wave of feminism that helped boost many women into prominence in the field at that time.

Needless to say, there are other versions of this story. And there are women writers who would rather die than acknowledge that feminism helped them in any way—even if only by bringing a lot of new female readers into a traditionally male genre, readers eager to buy and read the work of women writers.

Be that as it may, this is a new decade. It's fair to ask, where do I see myself now with regard to all this?

Well, I am *not* one of those women who makes haste, on panels and in print, to identify herself as "*Not*

a feminist" (God *forbid*, you can hear the nervous sub-
text). But I do understand the impulse.

The impulse is to avoid at all costs being trapped
by a label, boxed in in terms of what you may or may
not write about and still be deemed "politically correct," boxed out in terms of being spurned by readers,
editors, and other writers who have, alas, accepted some
narrow, fear-filled definition of the word "feminist"
with which *they* certainly don't want to be associated,
thank you very much; and no wonder when you look
at the definition they've bought.

All this is really a great pity. A useful term, which
simply has to do with the impulse to see and treat
women as full-fledged human beings with all of the
rights and duties thereof (check your Webster's), has
been captured and poisoned by the enemy. The word
"feminist" is now used most often to divide women
from their own interests and worse, against one another.

Many women writers will add to their disavowal of
feminism something like this: "I'm not pro-female, I'm
pro-*human*! I am a humanist, in the broad sense, and
I deal in human nature—*all* of it."

Unfortunately the humanist tradition, whose members historically have not been feminists but who currently like to think (and endlessly declare) that they
are for *everybody*, is hopelessly inadequate in just this
area. The vocabulary of prefeminist or nonfeminist dis-
course about human nature, no matter how "liberal"
or all-embracing in intention, is deeply imbued with
habits of thought and speech that routinely ignore or
denigrate the experience, understanding, and interests

of women in favor of those of men. Feminist scholars attest eloquently to their own constant struggles to stay alert to these habits and assumptions in their own writing.

This is not surprising. Outrageously sexist discussions have been carried on for generations under the false label of "objective scholarship," while actually serving the cultural purpose (among many others) of keeping women down.

At least now that particular purpose is subject to challenge, often by modern humanists of various academic stripes. But they are humanists with a feminist consciousness or they wouldn't think to raise the issue in the first place. And a humanist with a feminist consciousness is so vastly different from one without that to use the label "humanist" (or some looser phrase meaning the same thing) for both of them is futile and lazy. The gulf between them is simply too vast to be so blithely bridged, and you end up with outright falsehood or else a tangle of subdefinitions and justifications descending to absurdity.

If we're going to try to salvage a concept by redefining it, I'll take "feminist" over "humanist" any day. The former is in trouble, but is far less compromised than the latter with its long history of masculine bias. Besides, why resign "feminist," a perfectly good and useful word, to the narrow definitions and narrower purposes of the Radical Right or the Radical Left, thereby joining the Tremblingly Timid Middle in doing so?

Admittedly it's a lot more attractive to identify with the masculine (and therefore classy) intellectual tradition than with upstarts and troublemakers like Mary Daly or Dorothy Dinnerstein, say. However, you are then identifying with, for example, "The Ascent of Man" (a recent, entirely accurately titled and highly acclaimed television series on the history of civilization) and all that this implies.

Personally I consider that a high price to pay for not much value.

All this aside, the bottom line is that whatever values an author claims to hold or is accused of holding, her work inevitably demonstrates her true convictions. The question for me is not, "Is there a strong woman character in this story?" It's easy to write a deeply sexist story around a female protagonist and not even know it. Male writers do this all the time, and congratulate themselves for their own enlightenment, which women are expected to applaud.

No, my test is this: "Are there female characters of complexity, variety, and true importance to the protagonist of this story? Or is she or he *surrounded by and significantly connected only to males?*"

In other words, does the protagonist have a mother? Or sisters, women friends and confidantes, aunts, daughters, a grandmother? Female colleagues, enemies, lovers, rivals, teachers, you name it—as well as brothers, fathers, and so on? Does being human include (as it does in reality, whether it's acknowledged or not) important connections with *both* halves of the human race?

If not—okay. *Provided* there's a damn good reason in the story.

There hardly ever is. When women are omitted or included merely as tokens and caricatures, it's generally because the author doesn't believe that female people are worth her (or his) attention or the reader's.

You either see women as people, or you don't. Your work will tell.

So; am I a feminist? By my own lights, you bet I am, and proud of it. Self-respect as a woman in a misogynistic world is hard won, and I honor it in myself and in others where I find it.

Ah, but do I write feminist propaganda? By my own lights, no.

If I did, I would have forced myself to write Dr. Weyland as a female on political grounds, even though he lived in my imagination as a male. If I did, the Riding Women of *Motherlines* would be uniformly wise, creative, nurturing, and supportive, instead of all that as well as cruel, quarrelsome, coldly rational, and so on. Dorothea of *Dorothea Dreams* couldn't have a healing and fruitful love affair with Ricky because that is a personal rather than a political solution, and Valentine's wizard ally would automatically be a witch instead.

As things stand, I am certainly too feminist for some, not enough by half for others. I quit worrying about this when I realized that for me feminism is a point of view, not a party line. But what does that mean, in practical terms?

Well, none of this is in the front of my mind when I sit down to work. Writing a first draft is a creative act, not a critical one. If it's any good at all, the story spins itself out of the characters' hearts, not out of my rational and judgmental thoughts. But my convictions do make some decisions for me, before I put a word on paper.

So it would simply never occur to me to write about a woman-seducing vampire hunted down by a band of stalwart young men under the leadership of a wise old patriarch. Or the one about how the evil of birth control has taken over the world and has to be eradicated by a brave young man and "his" fecund woman. Or the one about the brilliant, beautiful woman scientist who abandons any interesting company she has (especially if it's female company) to subordinate herself gladly to an even more brilliant, not necessarily handsome, but usually older man. Or the one about the barbarians, which has no women in it at all except as background or loot. Or the one about how the great monster turns out to be Mom. Or the one about how being raped and enslaved and raped and enslaved is actually a dandy life for a girl—after all, it's "natural." Or the one (you fill in the blanks).

It would never occur to me, for one thing, because these stories are boring. They are heavily traveled highways to predictable ends, none of which is worth the journey.

It would never occur to me because such stories put women down. Too many women do that as it is, which is sad and embarrassing. Only a dope eagerly kicks herself in the head just because folks tell her that's the thing to do.

It would never occur to me because to write this brand of sexist propaganda—or *any* brand of propaganda—is to spit in the face of one's own talent. And that is a deadly error.

When you come up with a character who offers that treasure of true creativity, the unexpected, it's a criminal waste to force the character to do what is merely "correct" or acceptable according to a political formula, or a commercial one, for that matter—both of which provide "the" answers before the questions are even asked.

It's also self-limiting in the worst way: soon such characters, bouncing and fizzing with the unpredictability of life, stop coming around. As do readers with lively minds. There's nothing to attract them. Writing from "the" answers offers only the droning reassurance of the familiar—no questions, no surprises, no mystery.

No fun for the lively-minded writer, either. And if you stay in fiction writing without having fun, you are seriously cuckoo. The work is too hard and the rewards too uncertain for a sane person to stick with it on lesser terms.

For me, so far, the terms have been good. I may not know where I'm going, but in my dozen or so years of writing as a professional I've been fortunate enough to find my way, which I've tried to describe here: the way of making a road for yourself, out of questions, heading somewhere you don't recognize till you're more than halfway there.

This is the road of no-road, of improvisation and exploration, and it has the great virtue that no one can stake an exclusive claim to it, use it up, or wipe it out.

No-road is the most open road there is, maybe the only open road. Anyone can make it or take it if they so choose. To all lovers of the printed word, I recommend it.

Biographical Notes

Born and raised in New York City, Suzy McKee Charnas attended the High School of Music and Art and Barnard College, where she earned a degree in economic history. After graduating Ms. Charnas joined the Peace Corps and taught economics at the University of Ife in Nigeria. She spent several years teaching and traveling in Africa. It was at this time that Ms. Charnas began to write.

Ballantine published her first novel, *Walk to the End of the World*, in 1974. Suzy McKee Charnas currently resides in Albuqerque, New Mexico, with her husband Steven and their two children.

Books by Suzy McKee Charnas

The Silver Glove (Bantam Books, 1988)

Dorothea Dreams (Arbor House, 1986)

The Bronze King (Houghton Mifflin, 1985)

The Vampire Tapestry (Simon & Schuster, 1980)

Motherlines (Berkley Pub. Corp., 1978)

Walk to the End of the World (Berkley Pub. Corp., 1974)